How many of these Matt Christopher sports classics have you read?

Baseball

- ❑ Baseball Pals
- ❑ Catcher with a Glass Arm
- ❑ The Diamond Champs
- ❑ The Fox Steals Home
- ❑ Hard Drive to Short
- ❑ The Kid Who Only Hit Homers
- ❑ Look Who's Playing First Base
- ❑ Miracle at the Plate
- ❑ No Arm in Left Field
- ❑ Shortstop from Tokyo
- ❑ Too Hot to Handle
- ❑ The Year Mom Won the Pennant

Basketball

- ❑ The Basket Counts
- ❑ Johnny Long Legs
- ❑ Long Shot for Paul

Dirt Bike Racing

- ❑ Dirt Bike Racer
- ❑ Dirt Bike Runaway

Football

- ❑ Catch That Pass!
- ❑ The Counterfeit Tackle
- ❑ Football Fugitive
- ❑ The Great Quarterback Switch
- ❑ Tight End
- ❑ Touchdown for Tommy
- ❑ Tough to Tackle

Ice Hockey

- ❑ Face-Off
- ❑ Ice Magic

Soccer

- ❑ Soccer Halfback

Track

- ❑ Run, Billy, Run

All available in paperback from Little, Brown and Company

Skateboard Tough~~~

by Matt Christopher
Illustrated by Paul Casale

Little, Brown and Company
Boston   Toronto   London

Again to my wife, Cay

First Edition

Library of Congress Cataloging-in-Publication Data

Christopher, Matt.
    Skateboard tough / Matt Christopher. — 1st ed.
        p.   cm.
    Summary: When Brett's skateboarding abilities dramatically and inexplicably improve after using The Lizard, a skateboard mysteriously unearthed in his front yard, his friends start to wonder if the skateboard is haunted.
    ISBN 0-316-14247-6
    [1. Skateboarding — Fiction.   2. Mystery and detective stories.]
    I. Title.
PZ7.C458Sk   1991
[Fic] — dc20   90-49874

10 9 8 7 6 5 4 3 2

MV

Published simultaneously in Canada
by Little, Brown & Company (Canada) Limited

Printed in the United States of America

Acknowledgments

I wish to heartily thank skateboard enthusiasts Chad West, of Lake Wylie, South Carolina, and Michael Dickson, of Hopkins, South Carolina, for reading and approving the skateboarding portions of this book.

Skateboard
Tough

~ 1 ~

"HOLD IT! Hold it!"

Instantly, Brett wheelied to a stop, putting all his 121 pounds on his left foot, forcing the front end of "Cobra," his skateboard, to rise and the rear to scrape against the sidewalk.

His mouth parted as he started to say something, then he realized that the man hadn't yelled at him, but at the guy operating the digging machine. He was one of the workers constructing a foundation for the garage Brett's mother and father were having built in the backyard just beyond the driveway. Brett and his family hadn't lived in Springton long — only about six months — because of his father's change of jobs. One of the things his parents had always wanted was a new garage, and now, finally, they were getting it.

"What did you find?" the operator asked. Both he and the worker on the ground wore yellow coveralls and helmets.

"Some kind of box!" the worker yelled back, jumping down into the narrow trench that had been dug.

Curious, Brett skated onto the driveway toward the digging machine, hopped off the skateboard, and walked gingerly alongside the huge yellow monster to get a look at the box the enormous-toothed shovel had dredged up. The worker was lifting the box — a wooden one about a foot square and a yard long — out of the hole as Brett approached.

The man's broad, sweaty face broke into a smile as he looked up at Brett. "Know anything about this?" he asked, his voice a deep, throaty drawl.

"Not a thing," Brett said. "Can I take it?" he asked, reaching for the box with his gloved hands.

"Sure. It was on your property," the worker said, and handed it to him.

"Thanks," Brett said. He carried the box to the back stoop. Then he whipped off his gloves, flew into the house, and flew back out with a bristle brush, a hammer, and a screwdriver.

What could be in it? he wondered as he hurriedly brushed off the dirt that had stuck to the box. And why had somebody buried it there in the yard?

He felt eyes watching him from behind the screened door, and knew his mother was there, as anxious as he was to see what was inside the box. After he'd removed most of the dirt, he drove the screwdriver into the crack separating the nailed-down lid and the box proper. Little by little he got it loose. Finally, after pulling out the nails, he lifted off the lid.

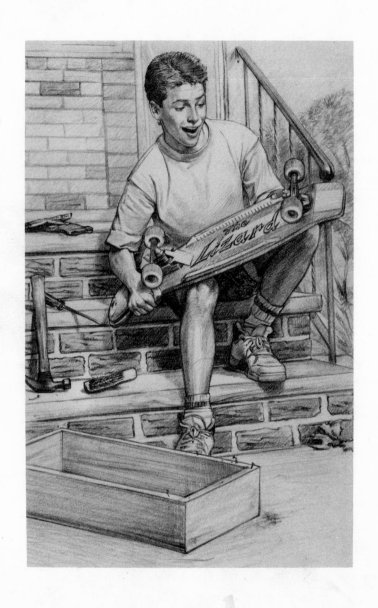

His eyes opened wide. A skateboard! A shiny blue-and-white-striped skateboard!

"I don't believe it." Mrs. Thyson's muffled voice came from behind the screened door. "Who'd bury a skateboard?"

"I don't know, Mom," Brett said, surprised and thrilled by the find. "But it's mine, now! And it's a double kick tail! Mine's just a kick tail." A double kick tail meant that both ends of a skateboard curved up, making it more effective for performing tricks.

Gingerly, as if it were a huge egg, he lifted out the skateboard and hefted it for weight and quality. His heart thumped with excitement.

"Mom, it feels great!" he whispered with awe. "Really great!"

Tenderly, he turned it over. "The Lizard" was imprinted in script between the trucks that held the urethane plastic wheels. Brett tried to guess how old the skateboard was. The worn wheels and ends showed that it had had plenty of use, but the shiny colors looked brand new, as though the board had been painted just before it had been placed into the box and buried.

"You're not going to keep it?" his mother said. "It doesn't seem right, you know."

Brett's heart sank a notch. He looked up at her, his brown eyes sad, like those of a pup that had just been denied a bone.

"Why not?" he said. "It was buried in *our* yard. Whoever buried it didn't want it anymore, right? What's wrong with my wanting to keep it?"

"I don't know. Maybe whoever buried it had a good reason. Maybe he — I assume it was a he — wouldn't want his skateboard ever to be used again."

Brett should have known his mother would put up a fuss. She wasn't crazy about his skateboarding in the first place. But he wasn't going to give up this beauty, no way.

"Maybe so, Mom," he said. "But that's his tough luck. It was in our yard and I'm going to keep it. That isn't all," he went on, jumping to his feet. "I'm going to ride it, too!"

Brett carried the skateboard to the driveway. After pulling on his gloves, he placed his left foot on the skateboard and pushed off with his right.

"What was in the box?" asked the worker who had found it.

"This board," Brett replied, coming to a halt. "I'm just going to try it out."

"Lucky for you that you like skateboarding," said the worker.

"Yeah, it *is* lucky," Brett said.

He shot a quick smile over his shoulder, then whisked down the driveway to the cement sidewalk, where he placed both feet on the board, came to an almost abrupt halt, spun the board in a complete 360-degree turn, then raced down the walk.

He did a wheelie — raising the nose wheels high off the sidewalk — then reversed the move, touching down the nose wheels and lifting the rear wheels. The board performed so noiselessly that Brett felt he was practically skating on a cushion of air. His own board, Cobra, never sounded as quiet nor skated as smoothly as The Lizard. With a board like this, Brett thought, I could become really good. I might even have a chance at becoming as good as Kyle.

Kyle Robinson was unquestionably the best skateboarder in Springton, and Kyle made sure everyone knew it. Brett would love to see someone challenge him someday, and who knew? Maybe with The Lizard, it would be him.

Brett's mind raced with thoughts of some of the tricks he could do, and several that he *wished* he could do. He also wished that there was somewhere he could go to practice in peace. Back in Ridgeville, his old town, there was a skateboarding arena, and twice a year the town sponsored a skateboard contest. But here in Springton, kids only had the side-walks — it was illegal to skate on the street —

and skating on sidewalks was no thrill, with pedestrians coming and going. They'd bore a hole through you with their mean glares.

Brett's thoughts were interrupted by the squeak of Mrs. Weatherspoon's high-backed chair as she rocked back and forth on her front stoop. Brett would swear that she spent ninety-eight percent of her life on that rickety old rocking chair. He knew from his mother that Mrs. Weatherspoon had no family nearby — her husband was dead, and her only daughter lived out of state — and he figured she was lonely. On an impulse, Brett waved to her, but she just continued to stare straight ahead. He guessed she didn't see him through the tinted lenses of her thick-framed glasses. Or maybe she was just unfriendly. Well, maybe if she were nicer, she'd make some friends . . . then she wouldn't have to spend all of her time by herself, sitting on the porch.

Putting Mrs. Weatherspoon out of his mind, Brett cut to the right, onto the curb, and headed back toward his home. He did an Ollie — positioning his front foot behind the front trucks of the skateboard, he pushed his back foot against its rear, then jumped up, the board hanging onto his feet as if it were glued to them, and landed with the tail of the board slamming against the walk.

He did it again, then whisked onto the curb and glided across it. Back on the sidewalk, a feeling of absolute confidence swept through him as he thought of a maneuver he had always wished he could do but had never tried — the Ho-ho, or handstand, standing with his hands on the board and his feet in the air. Just thinking about it used to scare him out of his wits.

Now, taking a deep breath, *he did it*, then flipped back onto the board with both feet. *All right!* he almost shouted. He had done it! He had finally done the Ho-ho!

His heart was filled with exultation now, an exultation he had never felt while riding his own skateboard. *This is heaven,* he thought, as he did the Ho-ho once again.

"Careful, wimp, or you'll break your back!" a voice yelled from the direction of the sidewalk.

At the sound of the familiar voice, Brett steered the board onto the street and flipped over onto his feet. But his aim was off and his left foot missed the deck, causing him to lose his balance and fall.

It was a good thing he knew how to fall, rolling over onto his back and then onto his feet with hardly a feeling of pain.

A laugh broke from the kid who had yelled at him, but by the time Brett had regained his feet, the kid, Kyle Robinson, was speeding down the sidewalk, his laughter trailing in his wake.

~ 2 ~

"OH, WOW! Hey, I never saw you skate like that before! Is that you, Brett Thyson, or somebody else?"

Brett gathered his wits together and saw a familiar face staring at him from almost the same spot where Kyle Robinson had first cried out to him. It was W. E. Winsor, all four feet two inches of him. Brett didn't know what W.E.'s real first name was, but W.E. stood for Walking Encyclopedia. He was only eleven, but he had a memory that everybody who knew him envied.

"W.E.!" Brett exclaimed, surprised. "Where'd you come from?"

"I was behind Kyle," W.E. said, standing straddle-legged on the sidewalk.

"Oh. I wish that guy would mind his own business," Brett mumbled, looking in the direction Kyle had gone.

"You don't like him very much, do you?"

Brett shrugged. "I don't know him that well. What bugs me is the way he's always showing off."

"He *is* a darn good skateboarder. I think you're just jealous," W.E. added, grinning.

"Maybe," Brett admitted, "but one of these days, I'd like to show *him* a thing or two."

"I don't know, Brett. Kyle's pretty good."

"Yeah. But I'll be better." Brett patted the board in his hand. "Now that I've got The Lizard, anything's possible."

W.E.'s eyes landed on the skateboard and stayed there. "When did you get *that*?" he asked.

"Maybe forty, forty-five minutes ago," Brett answered. "Why?"

"It looks used."

"It is," Brett said. "But it works great. Watch."

He rode the curb again for a few seconds, then burst into an 180-degree turn that he finished skating backwards. Seconds later he was dancing back and forth on the curb, and — as W.E.'s mouth fell open — Brett leaped across the short span of grass to the sidewalk, did a 360, and finished with a perfect two-point landing.

"Geez!" W.E. exclaimed, incredulous. "A Gator Slide, and an Ollie One-foot with a perfect three-hundred-and-sixty-degree pivot! Man, I didn't know you even *knew* those moves!"

"I didn't," Brett said, smiling.

W.E. stared at him. "Huh? You mean you just *did* them?"

Brett shrugged. "Well, I tried, and I did. And you saw me, right?"

"You bet your incredible moves I did!" W.E. said. "And when did you learn those grinds?"

16~

"Grinds?" Brett echoed. "I did grinds?"

"Look, don't tell me you did grinds — on that curb there — and didn't even know it?"

W.E. knelt before the board and studied it. "Something about this board looks awful familiar, Brett," he said, his voice more subdued now. "Where did you get it?"

Brett hesitated. For some reason, he was reluctant to say anything about where it had come from. But he should have guessed that someone — especially W.E. — would be curious about it.

Well, he could see nothing wrong in telling W.E. After all, he hadn't *stolen* the skateboard. It was rightfully his.

"It was in a box, buried in our yard," Brett explained. "I don't know who put it there, but it's mine now."

Brett waited for a reaction, but W.E. didn't say anything. He just slowly rose to his feet and moved back a couple of steps, still looking at the skateboard as if at any moment it might come alive.

~17

"What's the matter?" Brett asked. "Why that look?"

"I've seen that board before," W.E. said softly.

"Could be," Brett said with a shrug. He didn't want to hear any more. He wasn't interested in the skateboard's history. It was his now, and all he wanted to do was skate on it and enjoy it as much as he could.

"Well, you're going to see a lot of it from now on, because this board and I have some serious practicing to do. See you later, W.E." Brett zipped down the sidewalk, past Mrs. Weatherspoon's house again. He didn't bother to wave this time.

Reaching the curb, and seeing no cars coming, Brett bent his knees, grabbed both ends of the skateboard, leaped high, and did a complete 360 before landing on the street again. A feeling of extreme pleasure soared through him. It was only the second time he had ever done that trick.

Just wait, Kyle. One of these days . . .

He didn't see the woman and her small daughter until he was already on the sidewalk and the woman yelled, "Watch it, will you?"

Brett twisted to the left just in time to avoid hitting them. He jumped off the board, his heart pounding as he thought about what had almost happened. If he'd struck one of them, the skateboard might have caused a serious injury. He could have been sued for damages, and — worst of all — his skateboarding career would be over.

"I'm sorry," he said breathlessly.

"Sorry? What good is sorry? You almost ran into us! You should be more careful with that thing!" the woman declared hotly. She looked to be in her late twenties. Her blond-haired daughter was about three or four.

Brett nodded quickly, blushing with embarrassment. Being sorry wouldn't have done a bit of good if he had run into one of them. But he hadn't, and thank goodness for that.

There was no use standing there looking forlorn, either, Brett figured. It was a close call. Let it go at that. He vowed, though, that he'd be more careful from now on. Not that he hadn't been careful before. He always was. But sometimes close calls happened, he told himself.

He looked up the street, hoping he'd see his friend Johnee Kale. Maybe I can get Johnee to skateboard with me, Brett thought. Maybe I'll surprise him when he sees me pulling off some of my new tricks.

Brett's excitement over his newfound skill replaced any trace of worry about his near-collision, and he sprinted down to Johnee's house on the next block. He knocked on the door, and asked Johnee's older sister, who answered it, if Johnee was in.

"He's in the kitchen," she said, studying his face as she spoke. "You're . . . ?"

"Brett. Brett Thyson," he said. "We're new here, and Johnee an' I —"

"Oh, yeah!" she broke in. "Sorry I didn't recognize you . . ."

"Hey, Brett!" Johnee's voice rang out from behind his sister. "What's up?"

"Hi, Johnee," Brett greeted him. "Feel like skateboarding a little?"

Johnee was holding an almost empty glass of orange juice in his hand. "Sure! One sec!"

He drained the glass, put it in the sink, then raced out of the house with his black-trimmed orange skateboard. "Let's go!" he said.

He was so enthusiastic about leaving that he didn't even notice Brett's skateboard. Brett grinned as he followed his friend down the street, watching Johnee perform wheelies and Ollies. He felt lucky to have found a friend so soon, a friend who enjoyed skateboarding as much as he did.

They were crossing the street when Brett saw Johnee pull off a stunt that Brett had only seen in a magazine.

"Why, you son of a gun," Brett mused.

"Exactly my sentiments, Brett," said a familiar voice behind him. "It seems that your new friend, Johnee Kale, has learned a couple of new tricks, himself, doesn't it? That was a G-turn and a one-eighty Kick Flip."

Surprised, but not too surprised at the sound of the voice behind him — W.E. had a unique habit of sneaking up behind you like a cat — Brett smiled and nodded. "Yeah!"

Brett did a wheelie and a 180 Kick Flip himself. Then he spun and saw the human Walking Encyclopedia looking him directly in the eyes. "Do you want something?"

"I know why your skateboard seems familiar," W.E. said softly.

"You do? Why?"

"It belonged to a kid named Lance Hawker. He was a national skateboard champion by the time he was sixteen. People used to call him Crackerjack Hawker."

"A champion, huh? That's cool." Brett looked down at The Lizard with new appreciation.

22~

"Maybe some of it will rub off on me."

Brett's smile faded when he saw how serious W.E. looked. "What's the matter, W.E.?" A terrible thought struck Brett. "You think this Lance guy will want his board back? Well, it's mine now. I found it and —"

"No, Brett, he won't want it back," W.E. said solemnly. "He wouldn't have any use for it. He's dead."

~ 3 ~

"OH," BRETT said sheepishly. "I'm sorry. I mean, did you know him?"

W.E. shook his head. "I only know *of* him. Everybody in town used to talk about him. First because he won so many contests, and then because of the way he died."

Brett couldn't help feeling curious. "What happened?"

"It all happened a few years ago, at the height of Lance's career. He was hit by a car while skateboarding. That's why they made it illegal to skate in the streets here."

As usual, Brett noted, W.E. had all the facts, and he enjoyed sharing them. Brett looked down at The Lizard and felt a chill go through him. "Do you . . . do you think he was riding *this* board when . . . ?"

W.E. shrugged. "I don't know for sure, but it *was* his board, the one he used in all his contests."

Then Brett had another eerie thought. "He must have lived in my house."

"No, your house is brand new. The Hawkers lived around here, but their house was torn down a year ago, when they started building this development."

That's right, Brett remembered with some relief. His family was the first one ever to live in their house. Still, Lance couldn't have lived very far, because the board had been buried in their yard . . .

"Hey," Brett shouted suddenly. "Who buried The Lizard? It couldn't have been Lance, unless he buried it before the accident, but then why . . . ?"

"It could have been his parents," W.E. suggested. "Maybe it brought back bad memories."

"Maybe," Brett agreed. Then he asked, "Where are the Hawkers now?"

"They moved out of town soon after the accident," W.E. stated.

Brett heaved a sigh of relief. "Okay, then, no problem. Looks like I've got myself a new skateboard."

He started to take off in the direction of Johnee, but W.E. ran up and grabbed his arm. "You're not going to keep using it?" he asked, incredulous.

"Sure. Why not?"

"Doesn't it make you feel . . . well, creepy?"

Brett waved the idea away. "No. I'm sorry about what happened to the guy, but that's all in the past and it's not going to keep me off this board. It's ten times better than Cobra."

"What's better than Cobra?" Johnee appeared next to them, his forehead already covered with sweat from performing tricks on his skateboard.

Brett showed him The Lizard and, even

though he hated to do it, he explained to Johnee where the skateboard had come from and to whom it had once belonged.

Johnee was amazed. "Crackerjack Hawker himself? Man, he was really hot." He looked admiringly at The Lizard. "If that *was* his board, then I bet it's something special."

"It *is*." Brett grinned. Finally here was someone who appreciated his find. "Something about it really suits me. I've been doing all sorts of tricks I never could do before. W.E. knows what they're called, I don't."

Johnee didn't wait for W.E. to list them. "Okay, let's see some. Can you do this?"

With that, Johnee leaned down, grabbed the ends of his skateboard, and leaped over the narrow lawn to the curb, where he immediately performed a series of Frontside Grinds before jumping back onto the lawn and coming to a complete stop.

Brett followed Johnee's action to a T, bending down, grabbing the tips of his skateboard, leaping over onto the curb, and knocking off a few grinds before coming to a complete stop right next to Johnee.

"Looking good," Johnee said. "Maybe there *is* something about that board."

"Hey, how about giving the rider some credit?" Brett said, laughing. His laugh was cut short when he saw W.E. staring at him from across the street.

"Stop looking at me like that, W.E.," Brett said. "You make me nervous."

"Oh?" W.E. shrugged and smiled. "I'm sorry, Brett. But I just can't get over your . . ." He shrugged. "Your performance keeps amazing me."

He sounds more like a college professor than a kid, Brett thought.

"I'm glad," Brett said. "Then keep watching me. Maybe you'll see me doing tricks you've never seen done before."

"I wouldn't be surprised," W.E. replied.

Feeling an urge to try some more fancy tricks, Brett sped down the sidewalk. The

28~

skateboard glided across the walk with barely a whisper. It was so much quieter than his own, so much easier to ride and to balance himself on. Never would he return it to the grave where he had found it. It would be crazy. The board was too hot, too good to be left to rot.

His heart raced as fast as the skateboard as he came to the end of the block, leaped off, and zipped across the street. He took the curb, then skated along the curve of it, doing both Tail Wheelies (the front wheels lifting off the curb) and Nose Wheelies (the rear wheels lifting off the curb). The toughest part was maintaining his balance on the narrow curb without the wheels sliding off the side. But he was succeeding, and he was filled with pride as he zoomed up the street.

Suddenly, a sound ahead made him look up, and the thrill in his heart turned to alarm. Almost to panic. Skating toward him on the curb was Kyle Robinson!

Kyle was up to his usual tricks. He just had

to come along and show up everyone. Right now he was challenging Brett to a contest of guts, to see who would leap off the curb first in order to avoid a collision.

It won't be me, Brett thought. I'm going to stick it out to the very last.

Closer and closer they came, their speed not slacking a bit. And as the gap between them closed, the fear grew in Brett's heart. Will Kyle really stay on the curb, even if it means running into me? he wondered.

Neither one yelled out a warning. Both kept silent, each waiting for the other to make the move. Their eyes were on each other's now, trying to read the icy stares, waiting to see which one would show more fear and give in.

It won't be me, Brett kept telling himself. It won't be me.

But, at the last moment — at the very last instant before they would surely make contact and risk serious injury — Brett jumped off the curb.

He felt the wind brush his face as Kyle swept past him, laughing out loud, declaring his victory.

Brett stood on his skateboard, glaring back at Kyle, his breath coming in quick, sharp gasps. He felt angry at himself for giving in, and he tried to justify his action by telling himself that a collision would have been inevitable if he hadn't. Had he been wimpy? Or was the word "smart"? He preferred to think it was "smart."

"Hey, a new skateboard, huh?" Kyle said, wheeling around and skating back toward him. "Yours?"

"Of course," Brett said.

Kyle stepped off his board and took a step toward Brett's. "How about a ride?"

Brett pushed back a few feet. "Sorry. No one rides this baby but me."

Kyle shrugged, got back on his board, and pushed off down the street. He commenced doing a series of tricks, the first a simple and familiar one to Brett, one he had done himself. Kyle crouched down on his board with one leg stretched out straight ahead and his arms out at the sides. Other maneuvers included Ollies and curb tricks. Brett followed suit without a hitch.

Then Kyle went into fancier tricks, including a Ho-ho, which Brett duplicated without a bit of difficulty. Kyle went on to grind the front trucks of his skateboard on the edge of the curb, keeping the board parallel to the curb and its tail in the air. It was a trick Brett had never attempted before, but this time he was determined to try.

He followed Kyle's maneuvers and *pulled each one of them off perfectly.*

Well, not quite perfectly. On Kyle's last stunt, he somersaulted in the air and made a safe, two-footed landing back on his skateboard. Brett tried to do the same. But, at the very last moment, as he landed back on his skateboard, he lost his balance and fell.

"Careful, Brett," said Kyle mockingly as he swept around toward him. "Don't want you to get hurt."

"Don't worry, I won't," said Brett, brushing the street dirt off his padded knees and pants.

He watched Kyle speed away, and then turned back to W.E. and Johnee, who were staring at him from the sidewalk.

"Wowee, Brett," W.E. exclaimed, breathless. "That Shoot the Duck was simple. But you looked like a real pro pulling off a Ho-ho and a Nose Grind. When did you learn to do them?"

Ho-ho he understood. But Nose Grind? Boy, leave it to W.E. to know the crazy names of skateboard tricks! He never skated himself, but he sure knew every trick in the book, or close to it.

Brett wiped the sweat off his brow with his forearm. "Didn't know I had," he said.

"Yeah, sure," said Johnee. "You've been practicing behind my back."

"No, I haven't, I swear," said Brett. "I guess I'm just improving with age," he added with a smile.

"Well, don't go getting any older or someday you may catch up to me," Johnee said as he hopped on his board.

Brett and Johnee were always arguing about who was the better skater, but it was all in fun. Their friendly competition was nothing like Brett's rivalry with Kyle. When Kyle bragged about his abilities, he was serious, and everybody knew it. And, worse than that, he was right.

Brett pushed off and sailed down the sidewalk, with Johnee close behind. Despite his earlier fall, he felt pleased with himself. Just as W.E. had said, it was the first time Brett had ever performed those difficult tricks. He'd been reluctant to follow Kyle's every move at first, of course. Kyle was no amateur. But Brett had depended on The Lizard to do what he wanted to do, and it had worked. What a terrific feeling!

His good feeling was short-lived, however. Just a few seconds later his mother drove up and said she wanted him to come home right away.

"Oh, Mom!" he cried. "Do I have to? Johnee and I —"

"Brett," Mrs. Thyson said, in a tone he knew was serious, "there's been an accident."

Brett's stomach flopped. "What happened? Is it Shannon?"

"No, your sister's fine. It's one of the workers — the one who found that box."

~ 4 ~

BRETT LOOKED at the man's bandaged ankle — the left one — as the worker sat there on the back porch, a grim, disgusted look on his face.

Fortunately, the "accident" was nothing more serious than a sprain. But it was enough to upset Brett's mother. He figured she felt guilty that it had happened on their property. She'd even offered to make lunch for the men, and now she wanted Brett to pick up some food.

"How'd it happen?" Brett asked the worker.

"Got me. I was lifting one of those four-by-fours and slipped. The first time in my life. Can you beat that? But, like they say, there's always a first time. Right?"

"Right." Brett grinned.

"Happened right after I dug up that box," the man went on. "Guess that skateboard wasn't so lucky for me, eh?"

Brett wasn't amused by the comment. W.E.'s story about Lance Hawker was too fresh in his mind.

"Guess not," Brett said abruptly, and went into the house.

Mrs. Thyson yanked a sheet of long, narrow paper off the refrigerator door and handed it to him. On it was a list of groceries.

"Here," she said, giving him a twenty-dollar bill. "That should cover it."

Brett stuck the list and the bill into his shirt pocket and whisked out the door, figuring he could complete the errand sooner by taking his skateboard. Then, as if she were endowed with extrasensory perception, his mother called out to him, "And not on your skateboard! You walk!"

He paused, one foot just above the threshold, and looked back at her. "But, Mom," he pleaded, "it can't be more than a bag. Even if it's two —"

"You still walk," she cut him off short. He turned, half disgusted, half angry, and trounced out of the house and down the street, his hands pressed firmly into his pants pockets.

He didn't understand what she had against skateboarding. He always wore his protective gear, and he'd never gotten hurt. And with The Lizard, he felt more sure of himself than he ever had with Cobra.

Just thinking about The Lizard made him feel better. The board fit him so well it was almost like magic. But Brett knew magic had nothing to do with it. *He* was the one who rode it. *He* was the one who guided it to perform the tricks. *He* was its master.

He spotted Mrs. Weatherspoon on her stoop and looked away, feeling her beady eyes on him. She was beginning to give him the willies.

Arnie's Groceries was on the corner, two blocks down the street. Brett bought the groceries, and Mr. Wilcox — Arnie — piled them into two paper bags. Brett paid for them and left, carrying a sack in each arm. They're not heavy, thank goodness, he thought.

He stepped off the curb and was halfway across the street when someone behind him shouted, "Brett! Wait!"

He looked back and saw Kristyne Medler running across the street toward him, her brown hair bouncing on her shoulders.

"Hi," Brett said.

"Hi!" She reached for one of the bags. "Can I help you carry one?"

"Naw. I can carry 'em," he said. He could, but if she asked one more time . . .

"Please," she insisted. "I feel stupid walking here empty-handed."

Smiling, he handed her a bag. "If you insist," he said. "Thanks."

She was a year younger than he and in the seventh grade. But she was a good friend of Shannon's and she often came over to their house. Sometimes Brett wondered if she came to see Shannon or came to see him. It seemed that *he* was the one she wound up talking to most of the time.

His thoughts were interrupted by a familiar sound growing louder and louder behind him.

He turned and, sure enough, the sound was coming from a skateboard, and riding it was Kyle Robinson. A feeling of envy pierced Brett as he saw Kyle speed down the sidewalk toward them, then suddenly pull a wheelie and perform one Ollie after another without a pause.

"He's really good, isn't he?" Kristyne said, also fascinated by his tricks.

"Yeah," Brett said. "Really good."

An ache took hold of him and grew stronger and stronger, warping his mind. Good? I'm going to be good, too, he promised himself. A lot better than good. Just wait and see.

"Is Shannon home?" Kristyne asked.

"She was when I left to get the groceries," Brett answered. "Practicing her sax."

"Uh-oh. Do you think it would be okay if I stayed and waited for her to finish?"

Brett shrugged. "Sure. Maybe she's finished by now, anyway."

By the time they reached the house, Shannon *was* finished, and Brett was glad. He had better things to do than entertain Kristyne right now. He wanted to take off on The Lizard and meet up with Kyle Robinson.

Brett asked his mother for permission to go out and then took off, grabbing The Lizard and skating up the sidewalk to the spot where he had last seen Kyle.

But Kyle wasn't around. It wasn't like him, Brett thought. That guy seemed to have nothing to do but skate.

Suddenly there was a shout and a rush of air behind him. Just as Brett was about to turn around, his skateboard was kicked from under his feet, causing him to lose his balance and almost fall to the sidewalk. A dog appeared from somewhere and started to leap and bark its head off at him.

"Scram!" Brett shouted. "Git!"

The dog barked even louder.

Laughter broke out like some maniac's howl, and Brett turned to see that it came from none other than Kyle himself. He must have seen Brett coming, hidden behind a bush, then jumped Brett when he was off guard.

"You screwball," Brett grumbled as he hobbled after his skateboard, which had rolled off the walk onto the grass. Kyle stood some twenty feet away, arms crossed, laughing at him.

The front door of the house directly in front of them opened and a woman barged out, yelling, "Why don't you brats go home and mark up your own walks? You almost hit my dog, too! I saw that! Come here, Felix! Come here, pet, before they run you over!"

The dog rushed toward the front porch, changed its mind for a second, then ran up the steps and into the house, its tail wagging furiously.

Flashing one more glare at the boys, the woman retreated into the house and slammed the door behind her.

From the corner of his eye, Brett saw someone else watching them. It was Mrs. Weatherspoon, standing on the curb in front of her house. Brett felt himself flush with anger and embarrassment. What was she looking at? he thought. Why couldn't she go inside and quit spying on the neighborhood?

Kyle let out another peal of laughter and skated down the walk, performing wheelies and an Ollie, then a couple of tricks Brett could not name. Where's W.E. when you need him? Brett thought wryly.

Ignoring both the enraged woman and Mrs. Weatherspoon, Brett succeeded in imitating Kyle's tricks perfectly. He felt better with every move. He began to sweat, to feel an ache in the muscles of his arms and legs. Even in his back. But he wasn't losing his balance. He wasn't falling. He was doing each trick with the finesse of a professional.

I can be good, too, man. Real good, he told himself.

He saw Kyle turn up the street where he lived, but Brett kept going straight, heading for Springton Park. Once Kyle turned and waved to him, grinning mockingly.

Brett waved back. But he thought, Grin, wiseguy. One of these days I'm going to skate rings around you, and it won't be long now, either.

~ 5 ~

B RETT WAS disappointed to find Springton Park crowded with mothers and their
young children. While the mothers sat at the
picnic tables, the smaller kids rocked back
and forth on the large replicas of Walt Dis-
ney characters with all the gusto they could
muster.

The trouble was, the blacktop pavement was
almost fully occupied, too.

Isn't anybody with any kind of authority in
this town ever going to consider kids like
me who enjoy skateboarding? Brett thought.
Couldn't they turn one small corner of the
park into a skateboarding arena where skate-

boarders could skate to their hearts' content and not worry about running into someone? What could be so hard about that?

Nothing, Brett thought. It just takes someone with interest and initiative, that's all. Someone to take the bull by the horns.

But who is in a position to do that? Maybe an owner of one of the sporting goods stores in town, Brett reflected. Why haven't any of them come up with the idea?

The more he thought about it the more disgusted he became.

Finally, he saw a vacant space on the pavement not twenty feet away, right next to a concrete drain lined with a curving concrete wall. His troubled thoughts melted away. What a perfect spot for some neat tricks!

He raced to the vacant spot, wheelied to a stop, then leaped into the drain and landed with his front foot over the back wheel. He glided up the curve toward the pavement side, then zipped down into the depths of the drain and up the curved wall, his eyes on the nose of his board.

He raced to the top of the wall, lifted the tail and sailed along the coping, his knees bent, his hands stretched out to catch himself should he lose his balance and fall. But he didn't lose his balance. He didn't fall. He was performing like a veteran. His heart pounded. He had never felt so good. *He had just performed a trick he had never performed before in his life.*

He heard a cheer, and someone clapped. I guess someone else is enjoying this, too, Brett thought with pride.

He skated about fifteen feet along the coping, then shifted direction down the wall, putting the rear wheels of his skateboard down, and glided toward the bottom of the drain.

He whisked up on the other side, spinning near the top as he did so, and landed on the pavement with perfect ease.

He heard more applause, and a voice cried, "Geez, man! You're something, you know that? That was a Fastplant One-eighty Ollie!"

Brett grinned. He'd recognize that high-pitched voice anywhere.

"Hi, W.E.," he said, seeing the human Walking Encyclopedia sitting at a picnic bench under an old, gnarled oak. "How long you been there?"

"Long enough to see you perform those fantastic tricks," W.E. said, rising from the bench. His eyes lowered to Brett's skateboard and he shook his head. "You've really improved since you found that board."

"Thanks," Brett said, wiping the sweat off his brow with his forearm. Those tricky performances had sped up his circulation and made him hot.

"Doesn't it make you wonder? At least a little bit?" W.E. asked.

"Wonder? About what?"

"About how you've been able to perform

~49

such difficult tricks," W.E. replied. "Tricks you'd never even known about before."

"I must've seen them done somewhere," Brett said, feeling as though he had to justify himself. "Maybe I saw pictures in a magazine. Or some kid doing them on TV."

W.E. smiled. "Think so?"

Brett shrugged. "How else could I have been able to do them?"

"That's what I was thinking," W.E. said. "Ah . . ." He cleared his throat. "Have you really wondered about it, Brett?"

"About what?"

"The skateboard."

"Wonder about it? Why should I? It fits me perfectly, and I can skate on it better than I can on my other one. That's all I'm interested in, man."

"You don't think The Lizard has anything to do with . . . well, your skating? And with that worker almost getting killed?"

Brett stared at him. "What are you talking

about? That worker didn't almost get killed. He just sprained an ankle. And how could The Lizard have anything to do with *that*?"

You've lost your marbles, W.E., he wanted to add.

"Okay. But you just think about it sometime," W.E. said.

This time Brett did say it. "You've lost your marbles, W.E., you know that? You've really lost 'em."

Spinning around, Brett skated back into the drain and performed another 360-degree pivot. Remembering the maneuver W.E. had called the Nose Grind, he skated up the side of the wall, reached the coping, and turned up the tail of the skateboard just as another voice cut into his actions. "Okay, kid! Off that wall and git! This is no skateboarding arena!"

The voice of authority. Brett didn't have to look up to see who had ordered him off the premises. He leveled off the skateboard, zoomed down the wall, leaped onto the pavement, and wheelied to a stop in front of the park ranger. Brett nodded at the tall, broad-shouldered official wearing a brown uniform. Then he picked up his board and headed up the pavement toward home.

Remorse replaced his former enthusiasm. Here we go again, he thought. He'd been careful. Sure, he'd come close to running into that woman this morning, but he hadn't after all. And she could have done her share, too, by watching out for herself and her kid.

Anyway, that was the only time he had almost run into anybody. And he was going to make doubly sure it wouldn't happen again.

But look what happened. Along comes this big-shot park ranger and tells him to "git." As though he were a stray dog.

Once again he wished he could do something to convince people that kids like him needed a place to skate. An arena. But what could he do? Go to the town council? They'd laugh at him. There wasn't anything . . .

Then again, there *was* one thing he could do . . . write a letter to the editor of the *Springton Herald*! *That* might get somebody to start thinking.

Vowing to give it a try, Brett got back on his skateboard and headed toward home. He suddenly felt energized, and he couldn't wait to get his thoughts down on paper.

As Brett wheeled past Mrs. Weatherspoon's house, he noticed that she wasn't in her usual spot. Guess she finally got tired of staring into space, he thought, relieved that he didn't have to feel her ugly glare on him.

Brett's mother greeted him with an ugly glare of her own as soon as he walked in the door. Just looking at her pink-cheeked, unhappy face made him wish he had stayed out longer. Now what was wrong?

"I was wondering when you were coming home, young man," she lit into him. "I got a call from a woman up the street."

"Mrs. Weatherspoon?"

"I don't know. She didn't tell me her name. But she said that you and another boy were skateboarding in front of her house and that you almost ran into a dog with your skateboard."

It *had* to be that nosy old Mrs. Weatherspoon, Brett thought. That explained why she wasn't on her front porch — she was inside, phoning his mom.

"Look, Brett." His mother lifted a finger and shook it in front of his nose as if it were a weapon. "I'm not going to stand for any trouble from you because of your skateboarding. It seems to me that ever since that skateboard was dug up you haven't been off it for more than a minute. This is my last warning to you. One more incident like this — just one more, mind you — and that skateboard goes to the junkyard. Period!"

～6～

FOR THE next two days Brett didn't look at The Lizard even once, let alone skate on it. He was afraid that he might do something accidentally to give his mother an excuse to cart The Lizard to the junkyard.

One thing he couldn't get off his mind was Mrs. Weatherspoon. He knew she had squealed on him. But why? What had he ever done to her? She's just an old busybody, he thought angrily.

Since he wasn't out skateboarding, Brett had plenty of time to compose his letter to the editor of the *Herald*. As his family watched the evening news, Brett looked at the TV screen without seeing it. He was deep in thought.

"Well, no comment?"

He glanced at his father. "Sorry, Dad. What . . . ?"

"Didn't you hear that? Your Blue Jays just blew another one."

"Oh, they did?"

"That's what the man said. Weren't you listening?"

Brett shrugged, and shifted his position slightly on the lounging chair. "I guess I wasn't," he admitted.

"What have you got on your mind?" his father asked. "Let me guess. That skateboard. The Lizard."

Brett shrugged again. "Partly," he answered.

"Partly?"

"I've been thinking about writing a letter to the newspaper," he said.

"Oh? About what?"

"About somebody building a skateboarding rink in town."

56~

"A skateboarding rink?" his father echoed. "Hey! I think that's a terrific idea! Why not?" His voice quickly dropped. "But I doubt it'll work."

"You don't think I should write a letter?" Brett asked, disappointed.

"They might not even print it," his father said. "This town seems to frown on skateboarding."

"But that's because we skateboarders have no special place," Brett said, giving voice to all the arguments brewing in his head. "If we had a place to skateboard, we'd be off the streets. We wouldn't be a danger to other people, even though I don't think we're any more of a danger than kids who ride bikes, or motorbikes, or roller skates."

"I agree with your father," his mother cut in from her chair near the picture window. "It could be a waste of time."

Thanks, Mom, he wanted to say. I knew you'd be with me all the way. How she had consented to let his father buy him his first skateboard he'd never know. He must have caught her at a weak moment.

"Go for it, Brett," Shannon said. "If you don't, you'll never know."

She shot a glance at her mother right after she said that, as if she expected her mother to make some kind of harsh remark. But Mrs. Thyson just pursed her lips and turned her attention back to the TV set.

"I second that," Mr. Thyson said. "It's worth a shot. And we're proud of you for thinking of it, right, hon?" He looked at his wife, who acted as though she hadn't heard him.

Brett smiled, and got up. He excused himself and headed for his bedroom, eager to get going on the letter. He couldn't wait to tell the whole town — including his mother — that skateboarders could be responsible.

He cleared off a space on his small desk, got a pen and paper, thought for a bit, then began to write:

Dear Editor,

I'm one of the many kids in Springton who enjoy skateboarding, but there's no place for us to skateboard except on the sidewalks. And nobody wants us to skateboard on them. They say we're dangerous and cause a lot of trouble. So what can we do? Nothing!

But we're not going to do just nothing. We're going to keep skateboarding. Skateboarding has become a national sport. It's even become an international one. A lot of cities and towns have built special rinks for skateboarders. Why can't Springton do the same for its kids? If they did, then we would stay off the sidewalks. We wouldn't be a menace, like some people say we are. And we'd be happy.

I hope that you will print this letter, and that it will get somebody

to thinking about building us a rink.
There are fields for baseball, football,
and soccer. But there's not a single
place for skateboarding.

I hope that whoever reads this
letter will think about that.

Sincerely yours,

Brett Thyson

He read the letter over and felt satisfied
with it. Then he looked up the newspaper's
address, wrote it on an envelope, and put on
a stamp.

"It's finished," he told his parents on his way
out to mail the letter. He didn't want to wait
until tomorrow. He wanted the newspaper
editor to receive it as soon as possible.

"I guess you didn't want us to read it," his
father said, a faint smile coming over his face.

"It's not much," Brett said with a shrug.
"Anyway, if it's printed, you can read it then."
He headed for the door. "I'm going to mail it

now." Then, before his mother could say anything, he added, "I'm going on my bike."

There, Mom. Satisfied?

He stuck the letter inside his jacket pocket, opened the garage door, and got his bike. The Lizard was there on the bench, and he gave it a passing ᴉnce, as if he felt guilty for taking the bike instead of the skateboard. "Maybe tomorrow, Liz," he said half aloud.

It was quite a distance to the post office, fourteen blocks to be exact. He took his time riding there, staying as close to the right-side curb as possible, swinging out into the street only when there was a parked car in front of him. He passed the tennis courts, and noticed the crowd, the cars in the parking lot.

See what I mean, Mr. Editor? he thought. Even tennis players have their place; we should have ours.

He finally arrived at the post office, a sprawling brick building with half a dozen steps leading up to the double doors. He went

in and dropped the letter into the slot marked
STAMPED LETTERS.

There, he told himself proudly, I've done it.
I've written and mailed the letter. Now I can
only wait and see if it'll be printed and if
anybody will do anything about it.

He rode back the same way he had come,
so he could stop and watch some of the tennis
matches. His mother and father used to play
tennis, he remembered, then quit because his
mother started to get bothered by arthritis.
Brett had played some tennis himself before
he got into skateboarding. Once he switched,
he was hooked.

He watched for a while, then got back on
his bike and headed for home.

When he reached his block, something
caught his attention. Shannon was whiz-
zing around the corner on a skateboard. He
watched in disbelief — and then horror — as
she bumped into another kid riding his skateboard just as a blue truck blazed around the
corner.

~ 7 ~

"SHANNON!" BRETT screamed. "Oh, no!"

Shannon fell off her board as it hit the other kid's. The truck nearly hit them both, then swerved at the last minute and continued on, its horn blaring.

Brett's heart plunged to the bottom of his feet as he ran over to Shannon. The kid who had collided with her was none other than Kyle Robinson. Figures, Brett thought. Where there's trouble, there's Kyle. Brett noticed that Kyle hadn't even lost his balance during the incident, and now he just stood there, looking helplessly at Shannon.

Brett raced up to her side, laid his bike on the curb, and knelt down beside her. "Shannon! You hurt?"

"No, I'm . . . I'm all right," she said, gingerly lifting herself to her feet. She wiped her eyes with one hand, and rubbed her knees with the other.

"She ran into me," Kyle broke in before Brett could say anything. "She was coming around the corner. I saw her, but not in time. And that truck . . ."

Brett glanced down the street in the direction Kyle was pointing, but the truck was already out of sight. The driver probably had turned at the next intersection to prevent their reading his license number, Brett figured.

Once Brett realized that neither Shannon nor Kyle was hurt, he took a closer look at the board his sister had been riding. The Lizard! "Who told you you could borrow The Lizard?" he yelled at Shannon. "*Nobody* borrows The Lizard! Don't you understand that? Nobody!"

She shrank back from him as if afraid he was going to strike her. And he felt like striking her, too. She had no business . . .

From the corner of his eye he saw Kyle skate off down the street, glancing nervously over his shoulder. Chicken, Brett thought.

"I'm sorry," Shannon apologized. "I didn't think you'd mind."

"Well, I do mind," Brett said. "I don't want anybody . . . anybody," he added emphatically, "to ride The Lizard but me. Understand?"

He picked up the bike. "Here. You take the bike," he said. "I'll take The Lizard."

She nodded. She looked so apologetic that Brett almost felt sorry for her. But he couldn't let her know that. He wanted to make sure she would never borrow The Lizard again.

She took the bike and got on it.

Then her eyes darted past his shoulders, and at the same time Brett heard someone behind him.

He whirled, and saw Johnee and W.E. running toward them.

"You okay, Shan?" Johnee asked.

"I'm fine," Shannon said.

"We saw the accident," W.E. said. "We saw the whole thing."

Brett frowned. "So?"

"Shannon ran into Kyle, but it wasn't her fault," W.E. said.

"Look, W.E.," Brett said. "I know what you're thinking, and I don't want to hear it."

"I'm going to say it anyway, Brett, because it's true. It's the skateboard. It's The Lizard."

"No, it isn't! You're crazy! The Lizard has nothing to do with it!"

"What are you guys talking about?" Shannon asked.

"Oh," Brett said impatiently. "W.E. seems to think that this board is haunted or something."

Brett expected his sister to laugh at the idea, but she just stared at the board as though it were the first time she had ever laid eyes on it.

"*You* don't believe him, do you, Johnee?" Brett cried, anger reddening his cheeks and neck. "You don't believe that crock of bull, do you?"

Johnee met his eyes, but he said nothing. He seemed puzzled, uncertain.

"Okay! Okay!" Brett yelled hotly, skating away. "The heck with you guys! Believe what you want! It's not The Lizard! That's dumb! *Dumb!* Come on, Shan! Let's get out of here!"

He headed for home on The Lizard and Shannon followed him on the bike.

I can't believe those guys, Brett thought bitterly. Especially W.E., spreading crazy stories about me. Why can't he just face facts? The Lizard isn't hexed, it's just a fantastic board. After all, it *did* belong to a champion . . .

The thought of Lance Hawker — and how he died — sent chills up Brett's spine despite himself. What if the same thing had happened to Shannon?

As if she read his mind, Shannon said, "Shall we tell Mom about the accident?"

"No," Brett said quickly. She was the *last* person he wanted to tell. She'd throw The Lizard out for sure. "It would just worry her. Mom's got enough worries to keep her busy for a month."

Shannon nodded knowingly. "But what if she asks me about my knees? You've got to be blind not to see those scratches."

"Just tell her you slipped on a banana peel," he said, laughing.

"Oh, sure," she said.

Brett stopped laughing when he remembered how mad he was about her taking The Lizard without permission.

"Why did you take The Lizard, anyway?" he asked her. "Why didn't you take Cobra?"

She shrugged. "I don't know. I guess I . . . just wanted to try The Lizard out."

"I guess you did," Brett said.

He was glad to put The Lizard away in the garage when they reached home. Haunted or not, he'd had enough of it for one night.

On Friday, it looked as though Brett's luck had changed — this time for the better. He got a phone call from a member of the *Springton Herald*'s staff. She informed him that his letter had been received and asked if he really was the one who had written it.

His heart almost leaped out of his chest. He had begun to think that the letter had been completely ignored or lost.

"Yes, I wrote it," he said nervously.

"And you live at eleven thirty-nine Valley Hill Road?" the woman asked.

"That's right," Brett answered.

"Thank you," replied the caller, and hung up.

She didn't even give him a chance to ask if they were going to publish the letter!

Did that call mean that they *were* going to print it?

His question was answered the next morning, when he saw his letter in the paper. How about that? he thought, reading it again and again and feeling better each time.

"Mom! Shannon! Look!" he cried. "They printed my letter in the paper!"

They read it together.

"That sounds good," said his mother, but she didn't seem very enthusiastic. "I hope somebody reads it."

You're really encouraging, Mom, you know that? Brett wanted to say to her. But he didn't bother; it was pointless to argue. Instead he grabbed the newspaper and took off for Johnee's house. If anyone would be impressed by his letter, Johnee would.

~ 8 ~

"YOU'RE REALLY serious about this, aren't you?" Johnee asked after he read the letter. They were sitting on the front steps of the Kales' house.

"Yeah. Aren't you? I thought you loved skateboarding," Brett said, a little disappointed by his friend's cool reaction.

Johnee shrugged. "I like it, but there are other things in life."

"But wouldn't it be great to have an arena in town?" Brett coaxed.

"Sure it would. I just doubt it's gonna happen. Especially after what happened to Lance. . . ." Johnee's eyes dropped down to The Lizard, on the step next to Brett.

Brett snorted. "I'm sick of hearing that old excuse. An arena would prevent accidents like that from happening."

"Yeah, I know. But I don't know if anyone is going to listen. There aren't many people who feel as strongly as you do."

"There's Kyle Robinson," Brett offered with a smile.

"That's right," Johnee agreed, grinning. "He probably sleeps on his skateboard! But it pays off — look how good he is."

"He's good, but I'm better."

"What? Nobody's better than Kyle, man."

"You haven't seen me skate lately. I can do all sorts of new tricks." Brett got up to demonstrate.

Johnee held up his hand. "You don't have to show me. I've seen you, and you are getting better —"

Brett whirled around sharply. "I'm the *best!* I'm telling you!"

"Okay, okay," Johnee said. "Chill out, man. It's not that big a deal."

"Maybe it isn't to you, but it is to me. I want to put Kyle in his place once and for all." Brett pounded his leg with his fist as he spoke.

"How are you going to do that?" Johnee asked.

"I don't know," Brett said, sounding deflated. "But Lizard and I will find a way."

Johnee shook his head. "You and that board. Maybe you were better off without it."

"What does everyone have against this board?" Brett said angrily. "Don't tell me you believe what W.E.'s been saying."

"All I know is, you seem obsessed with it," said Johnee.

"No way!" said Brett. Then, in a softer tone, he said, "It's just an excellent board, nothing more."

Brett moved out into the street and stepped onto The Lizard. "Come on, man. Let's do some tricks."

"Can't," Johnee said, standing up. "I've got some chores to do. Maybe later."

Brett felt another wave of annoyance wash

over him. What was with Johnee? Didn't he like to skate anymore? Well, if he doesn't, Brett thought, I'll go find someone who does. Maybe even Kyle.

"Later, man," Brett said, taking off.

First my mother, then W.E., and now even Johnee. Everyone's on my back, Brett thought angrily as he wheeled down the street. *And for what? Just skateboarding. It's not like I'm selling drugs or anything.*

As he started to go past Mrs. Weatherspoon's house, a cab pulled up at the curb and she got out, carrying two suitcases.

And here's another one, old snitch Weatherspoon, Brett fumed. He noticed that she was struggling to carry the bags up the walk, but he didn't offer to help. She could shift for herself. He pretended he hadn't seen her and went on.

But she called out to him. "Excuse me."

Brett considered not stopping, but then thought better of it. He didn't want her to get him into more trouble with his mom.

74~

"Aren't you Brett Thyson?" she asked.

Brett nodded curtly. Yeah, the one you ratted on, remember? he said silently.

"I thought so." She put down the suitcases and walked toward him. "I saw your letter in this morning's paper."

Brett didn't respond, unsure of what she wanted from him. Was she going to tell him she hated his idea?

"It was a good letter. Very well written, and from the heart," she went on.

"Uh, thanks," Brett stammered. Was this really Mrs. Weatherspoon, or a twin coming to visit?

"Oh well, I'll let you get going. I'm sure you're anxious to get back on that skateboard." She smiled and — to Brett's surprise — even winked. "You're very good — I've seen you."

"Thanks," Brett repeated lamely. Once he recovered from his shock, he said, "Can I help you with your bags?"

She looked down at them. "Oh, that would be very nice. I can get this one, if you'll carry that one." She pointed to the smaller suitcase, but Brett picked up the larger one.

"I don't know why I brought so much for just one week," she said apologetically as they walked up the steps to the door. "I was visiting my daughter and grandchildren. It was so good to see them again."

Brett nodded politely. The visit certainly must have been good for her — it had changed her personality!

When they reached the door Brett said good-bye and started to leave.

"Well, thank you, Brett," Mrs. Weatherspoon said. "It was awfully nice of you to welcome me home like this." She thought for a moment and then added, "Come to think of it, you ushered me off, too."

"Huh?" Brett stopped in his tracks and looked back at her, confused.

"Just before my cab arrived I saw that little

run-in you had with Mrs. Brisby's dog," Mrs. Weatherspoon said.

Brett blushed. "Yeah, my mother told me you called. I'm sorry —"

"Oh, I'm afraid she must be mistaken. I didn't call. I didn't have time. And anyway," she added with a mischievous chuckle, "I don't much care for that dog anyway."

Brett laughed, in surprise and relief. So it must have been Mrs. Brisby herself who had called. And all this time he thought Mrs. Weatherspoon . . . Well, it was obvious that he had been all wrong about her.

"I won't tell if you won't," Brett said.

"Deal." Then she waved him off. "Thank you again, Brett. You should drop by more often. And I hope your letter brings some results."

Me too, thought Brett, feeling a hundred times better. The whole world wasn't against him after all!

~ 9 ~

OVER THE next few weeks, Brett spent most of his time alone with The Lizard, practicing his moves. He tried to stay out of his mother's way around the house, and he was careful to skate in uncrowded areas, so that she wouldn't have any more opportunities to yell at him. He didn't see much of Johnee, either. Johnee was spending more and more time with W.E., and Brett didn't want to hear any more of his stupid theories about the skateboard. He just wanted to ride it and sharpen his skills so that he could take Kyle's place as the best skater in Springton.

Brett's hard work was paying off, too. He

and the board had become one; it responded so quickly to the slightest touch that Brett felt as though it could read his thoughts. His moves were smooth and effortless, and he rarely lost his balance, even during the most complicated tricks.

Passersby who saw Brett perform his feats often applauded and remarked on his talent. A few of them asked his name and linked him to his letter in the *Herald*. But no one offered to do anything about his suggestion, and Brett had come to grips with the fact that his parents were right about Springton's attitude toward skateboarding.

One morning, while he was eating breakfast, Brett heard the harsh, grinding sounds of a truck and other heavy equipment not too far away.

"What's going on out there?" he asked his mother. "Are they building another house?" Ever since the Thysons had moved in, new construction of one sort or another had been going on in their neighborhood.

His mother stepped outside for a moment and returned with a puzzled look on her face. "I don't know what it is exactly," she said, "but it looks as if something is happening down on the corner."

Brett wiped his mouth with a napkin, then went out to investigate. At the corner where Mrs. Weatherspoon lived, he saw a truck and a bulldozer. It appeared that Mrs. Weatherspoon was having something done to her backyard. Brett wondered why she was bothering, since she spent all her time on the front stoop. He thought about going down to ask her — she *had* invited him to drop by, after all — but he decided against it. He had better things to do, namely practicing with The Lizard.

He went back inside, closing the door against the loud, raucous sounds.

The next day they were at it again.

By now Brett was piqued by curiosity, and he walked over to see what the workers were up to. He came to an abrupt stop the minute he saw Mrs. Weatherspoon's yard. They were blacktopping it!

Brett stared, unable to believe his eyes. Why in heaven's name would someone blacktop a perfectly beautiful yard?

Poor Mrs. Weatherspoon, Brett thought. Maybe she was becoming senile. That was the only explanation he could come up with for her strange behavior . . . unless she just didn't like grass, or she was tired of having to take care of it. Yes, that must be it, he concluded. Without a family around to help, it was too hard for her to maintain a lawn. If only he'd known, he could have offered to help. Oh, well, it was too late now . . .

"Brett." A voice interrupted his thoughts.

He glanced up at the stoop, his eyes going first to the rocking chair where Mrs. Weatherspoon so often sat. It was empty.

Then he saw her in the doorway. She was smiling and beckoning to him. At least she doesn't seem to regret her decision, Brett thought.

"Can you come here a minute?" she asked softly.

"Sure," he said, and ran up the steps.

Mrs. Weatherspoon stepped out onto the stoop, closing the door gently behind her. Her smile broadened. "Do you know what's being done in my backyard?" she asked.

"It looks like you're having it covered," Brett said.

"Well, part of it anyway. But do you know why?"

He shook his head. "I — I have no idea," he answered.

"None at all?" She was strangely excited, like a kid with a big secret.

"No."

"I got to thinking about that letter you wrote," she said.

"Yes," he said, puzzled. What did his letter have to do with anything? Then Brett's heart began to pound, as an answer came to him. Could it be . . . ?

Her words filtered through his thoughts.

"That huge backyard of mine is just sitting there, growing grass and weeds. Why not do something worthwhile with some of it? Why not make it into something that kids who are crazy about skateboarding, and have no place to skateboard — just as you wrote in your letter — can use? So . . ."

"Mrs. Weatherspoon!" Brett cried, filled with the most joyous feeling he'd had in all his life. "You're building a skateboarding rink? That's great! Oh, that's just great, Mrs. Weatherspoon! You're wonderful, you know that? You're really wonderful!"

He was so excited that he threw his arms around her and gave her a great big hug. Then he stepped back, suddenly embarrassed, but Mrs. Weatherspoon was beaming.

"I take it you are in favor of the idea?" she said.

"You bet! I can't wait to try it out!"

"Well, now, it won't be finished for a few more days. Do you think you can wait until then?"

Brett nodded. "I've waited this long, what's a few more days? But can I tell everybody about it?"

"I guess there's no harm in that," she said. "I just hope I'll be able to handle the crowds when the time comes." Mrs. Weatherspoon winked at him.

"Maybe I won't tell *every*body," Brett said, thinking of Kyle. "Maybe it should be a surprise to some people."

He raced home and told his family the good news. His parents were amazed.

"It takes a lot of money to do something like that," his father said. "Just the insurance alone . . ."

"It's very generous of her," Brett's mother agreed. "I sure wouldn't do it."

We know that, Mom, Brett thought. But he wouldn't let her put a damper on his enthusiasm.

Even Shannon was excited. She asked Brett if she could use his old board, Cobra, when the arena was ready.

"Oh no, not another one!" Mrs. Thyson cried, her hands to her head.

It took a few more days for the workers to finish the blacktop, because special bumps, curbs, and banked sides had to be included. Then a six-foot-high chain-link fence was built around it. Mrs. Weatherspoon was wise to do that, Brett thought, to keep every kid, cat, and dog in the neighborhood from overrunning the place.

Brett was there when the last bolt was tightened, when the men cleaned up the mess they had made and drove away, leaving the blacktopped arena looking clean, shiny, and ready for action.

But that wasn't all. Two more men arrived, each carrying a wooden ramp. "Where do you want these?" one of them asked Brett.

Brett thought a minute, then said, "One on each side."

The men placed the ramps on opposite sides

of the rink. One of them said, "Have a good skate," as they walked out.

"Well, it's ready, Brett," Mrs. Weatherspoon said, admiring it alongside him. "It's ready for you, and for your friends."

His heart thumped like a clock gone mad. "Oh, Mrs. Weatherspoon, I can hardly believe my eyes. This is what I've dreamed about, what I was wishing somebody would do. Only I never dreamed it would be you, Mrs. Weatherspoon. You're the best." He paused, tears choking his throat. "I'll call up some of my friends, and I'll be back with my skateboard."

Mrs. Weatherspoon gave him a pat on the back. "You do that," she said. "Meanwhile, I'll bring my chair back here."

He sped home, phoned a few guys — even W.E. — then got The Lizard and skated over to Mrs. Weatherspoon's backyard.

The brand-new blacktop was terrific to skate on. Brett did a dozen various freestyle tricks while Mrs. Weatherspoon sat on the stoop, watching him. He was alone so far, the first kid ever to skate on her rink, and it looked as though she was enjoying herself as much as he was. Who would've known that behind that quiet, solemn face lurked one of the kindest, most generous persons he'd ever known?

He did a Gymnast Plant on a ramp, then a High Air, launching as high as he could off the edge of the ramp; his landing was greeted by an explosion of sound from the entrance of the rink. Wheeling to a stop, he saw that some of the guys had arrived and were giving him a hand for the High Air.

He laughed, and waved them in.

"Hey! This is great!" one of the guys cried, pushing off on his skateboard and going into a trick. Others echoed the cry.

"Thank that lady over there!" Brett yelled, pointing at Mrs. Weatherspoon. "This is her place!"

"Thanks, Mrs. Weatherspoon!" the guys all yelled at the same time.

She just sat there, answering their thanks with a pleased smile and a gentle wave of her hand.

"Just be careful," she cautioned.

"Don't worry! We will!" they replied.

Brett wasn't surprised when he saw W.E. introduce himself to Mrs. Weatherspoon and sit down beside her. No doubt, knowing W.E.'s talkative nature, they'd become good friends in no time. Mrs. Weatherspoon would probably learn more about skateboarding than she ever cared to, Brett mused.

In seconds, half a dozen kids were performing tricks on the blacktopped surface and on the ramps. The sound of their wheels and trucks was music to Brett's ears, and he wondered if Mrs. Weatherspoon shared his feeling. It certainly looked that way.

Brett saw a familiar face looking on from the gate that led into the yard. He stopped in the middle of a Kick Turn and motioned to Johnee Kale to come and join them.

Johnee hesitated for a few seconds, then he put one foot onto his skateboard and pushed off. In no time he was performing wheelies, Ho-ho's, and Shoot the Ducks.

"Isn't this great?" Brett called to him.

"It's super!" Johnee cried happily, swinging into a One-Wheel 360.

Brett grinned as he watched him, then duplicated the move and sprang into another, a two-handed handstand and then a Hand Plant. Then he leaned down, grabbed the ends of his skateboard, and *did a complete somersault*, landing perfectly back on the blacktop without losing his balance.

Whistles, cheers, and applause greeted him as he pushed off toward a vacant ramp, zoomed up on it, and performed a 360 aerial, a complete spin in the air, similar to the somersault, but much higher.

Again applause followed.

Johnee and Brett exchanged a high five, then Johnee's eyes swept past Brett's left shoulder. "Hey, look who just came in. Your old buddy."

Brett turned. "Yeah," he said, as he saw Kyle Robinson coming in with his skateboard. "Guess we made so much noise he couldn't help but hear it."

He almost wished that Mrs. Weatherspoon wouldn't let Kyle in, but she didn't know him any more or less than she knew the other kids. They were all skateboarders to her.

"Join in, young man," she invited him. "Let's see what you can do. Just don't do anything too fancy that might get you hurt, that's all I ask."

"Thanks, ma'am," Kyle said, and pushed off onto the rink.

"Punk." Brett snorted, and headed toward one of the ramps. He shot up on it, and landed backwards on the blacktop after twisting The Lizard into a 180-degree turn.

"Brett!" he heard a shrill voice cry out. "Oh, Brett!"

"Mrs. Weatherspoon's calling you," one of the kids said.

Brett wheelied to a stop and saw her motioning to him. Wondering what she wanted, he shot off toward her. "Yes, Mrs. Weatherspoon?" he asked as he came to an abrupt stop in front of her.

She leaned forward and said softly, her voice low enough that only he could hear it, "Brett, I couldn't help noticing the look you gave that boy who just came in. I've seen him before, and I've noticed that he's a good skateboarder. Very good. Yet, that look . . . Is there something that . . . ?"

"No," he said, before she went any further. "There's nothing. We just . . ." He shrugged, and forced a smile. "He's okay, I guess."

"You guess?" Her eyebrows arched.

"No. He's okay. And like you said, he's good. Real good."

She gave him a smile and tapped him on the shoulder. "All right, Brett. Go on and skate. You're not bad yourself, you know."

He flashed a smile, and felt his face flush up just a little. "Thanks, Mrs. Weatherspoon," he said, and got back on his skateboard and skated away.

She was sharp, he told himself, to have made that observation about him and Kyle. Brett was glad that he hadn't said more about Kyle. He knew Mrs. Weatherspoon wouldn't approve. Now that he thought about it, he was glad, too, that Kyle had found out about the arena. Now people would have a chance to compare them, and everyone would see that Brett was the better skateboarder.

After half an hour or so, Mrs. Weatherspoon stood up and clapped her hands to get everyone's attention.

"I'm sorry, kids," she said, "but, as you must realize, we ought to have a time schedule for this. I think from ten o'clock to twelve, and from two to four, don't you? What's your opinion?"

They clapped and yelled. "Great, Mrs. Weatherspoon! That's super!"

"Good," she said. "So it'll be those hours every day of the week. Well," she went on, glancing at her wristwatch, "it's now three-fifteen. You have forty-five more minutes. Then home you go!"

"Okay, Mrs. Weatherspoon! Thanks!" the guys cried as she turned and went into the house.

"Isn't she a fantastic lady?" Brett said to Johnee as the door closed behind her.

"Who would've guessed?" Johnee said.

When four o'clock rolled around, Brett was worn out from skating, and happier than he'd been in a long time. The arena was perfect for performing tricks, and Brett had pulled off all of his without a hitch.

He knew the guys were talking about his talent, and he'd even seen Kyle watching him with a strange expression on his face. Could it have been envy? Or was it worry?

Well, you *should* be worried, Brett thought as he and the others headed home. *Your number is up, Kyle Robinson.*

~ 10 ~

JUST WHEN Brett thought life couldn't get any better, it did. Two days later, Brett got a call from W.E.

"Good news!" W.E. said. "Mrs. Weatherspoon has come through again!"

"What do you mean? What did she do this time?"

"Well, I had quite a talk with her the day you guys tried out her arena," W.E. explained. "And you wouldn't believe what she's offered to do."

"What?" Brett said, growing impatient.

"How'd you like to compete in a contest?"

Brett caught his breath. "You're kidding."

"A contest is too serious to kid about, old buddy," W.E. said. "And, know what? She asked *me* to do the arranging, including the advertising."

Brett wasn't surprised. "You're the perfect guy for the job," he said. "Got the date planned yet?"

"It's two weeks from Saturday."

"Wow, that's soon," Brett said, already thinking about the routine he'd have to put together between now and then.

"I don't think you have to worry about practicing," W.E. said with a chuckle. "The contest is really just for you and Kyle, you know."

"What do you mean?"

"Mrs. Weatherspoon asked me about you and Kyle," W.E. explained. "After I told her about the rivalry between you two guys, she thought a contest would be a good idea."

"*She* did?"

"That's what I said."

You and your big mouth, Brett thought to himself. But he had to admit that an official contest — in front of a big crowd — was just what he wanted. Then Brett had a more worrisome thought. "W.E., did you say anything else to her?"

"About what?"

"About . . . anything."

"You mean about The Lizard?"

"Yeah."

"No, I didn't. She'd never believe me, anyway." He paused a moment, then asked, "Do you, Brett?"

Brett snorted. "Of course not. I think you've let skateboarding go to your brain." Then he added, "Got a question for you, W.E. You enjoy skateboarding so much, why don't you ever do it? Don't tell me you can't afford one. I've seen your father's Caddie."

"I'm not the athletic type," W.E. admitted frankly. "Besides, I like being a statistician better. I want to be a sportscaster someday."

"Hey, that's not a bad idea! You might be announcing those Braves games! Okay, W.E. Thanks for calling. I'll see you around. Oh, what time's the contest?"

"Two P.M. You'll have to sign up for it by next Friday night. I'll bring an application to you tomorrow. We're going to have both a Beginners Division and an Advanced Division contest. Mrs. Weatherspoon thought it would be good to do it that way so that little kids can compete, too."

"What class do you think I should sign up for?" Brett asked, cracking a smile.

"Tell you one thing: If you sign up for the Beginners Division, you'll be eliminated before you even start," W.E. replied, and laughed.

Brett laughed, too, thanked W.E. for all he and Mrs. Weatherspoon were doing, and hung up.

Good old Mrs. Weatherspoon, he thought. She was coming through again, just like W.E. had said. And the reason she wanted to sponsor a contest was because of him. Who would have thought his rivalry with Kyle would be so important to an old woman that she would up and do a thing like this?

"What was that all about?" Mrs. Thyson asked as Brett headed into the living room, still floating on air.

"You wouldn't believe it, Mom," he said, and explained it all to her, except *why* Mrs. Weatherspoon was putting on the contest. No need to go into that.

"Let me get this straight," Mrs. Thyson said when Brett had finished. "Mrs. Weatherspoon is going to hold this contest by herself?"

"Well, yeah," he said, beginning to feel uncomfortable under her piercing gaze. "But we — the guys — will help her. W.E. is spreading the word —"

"That's not what I'm concerned about," Mrs. Thyson cut in. "How will she judge it? Does she know anything about skateboarding? What about safety?"

"Oh, Mom," Brett said with a sigh. "It's not

~99

that big a deal. It's just a little contest, for fun."

But Mrs. Thyson wasn't convinced. "I don't know. I just don't think it's a good idea."

All of Brett's earlier excitement wilted and he felt anger growing in its place. Why had he told her about the contest? She didn't understand anything, and she was determined to take away any pleasure he got out of skateboarding.

"Just forget it, Mom!" he exploded. "You know, I think Mrs. Weatherspoon cares more about me than you do!" He spun on his heels and stormed out the front door.

Brett flung open the garage door and grabbed The Lizard. As he propelled himself down the street and away from his house with strong pumps of his foot, he calmed down. He surrendered himself to the board, spinning and doing wheelies until his head was clear again. Skating was what he enjoyed most and did best, and he knew it wasn't wrong.

He knew, too, that the contest *was* a good idea. He would do everything he could to make sure it happened, and to make sure he won first place. He'd do all of his fancy tricks — and maybe even some that he hadn't tried yet, some extra-special, stupendous moves that would knock everyone's socks off. Especially Kyle Robinson's.

Brett turned around sharply and headed toward the town library. He was sure to find some sports magazines there that showed the latest in skateboarding stunts.

With the help of a librarian, Brett located the information he needed, and more. As he flipped through the pages of one of the older magazines, he saw a photograph of a teenager sailing through the air on a skateboard. The caption underneath read: "Crackerjack Hawker, National Freestyle Champion."

Brett's pulse quickened as he examined the photo more closely, trying to get a bead on the boy he had heard so much about. Was that

The Lizard he was riding? The angle of the photograph made it hard to tell, but the board was the right shape, and it was a double kick tail. . . .

Again Brett wondered who had buried The Lizard, and why. He couldn't help thinking about W.E. and his theory about the board, that it was somehow hexed. It was a strange and stupid thing to believe, especially for someone as smart as W.E. But, Brett had to admit, his life had certainly changed since the day he had opened that wooden box. Did Lance bury the board because he, too, believed it was hexed?

Hoping to learn more about The Lizard and its previous owner, Brett read the article. There weren't many facts specifically about Lance, only that he rose to fame quickly because of his amazing ability, and that skateboarding was his life. He toured the country for weeks on end to compete in contests and perform in exhibitions for charity. It didn't sound half bad to Brett — he could understand someone's wanting to spend most of his time on a board, perfecting his skill.

Brett turned back to the photograph of Lance and studied it again. He looked a few years older than Brett, and he was wearing long black spandex shorts and a bright yellow T-shirt with the number six on it. In a way, Brett wished he had known Lance. They would have had a lot in common.

Brett carried the magazine over to the copier and duplicated the photo. Then he folded it carefully and stuck it in his wallet before putting the magazine back on the shelf.

~ 11 ~

THE NEXT morning, Brett decided he wanted to do something to show Mrs. Weatherspoon his appreciation. Only he didn't know exactly what to do. He waited until his mother was out of earshot — he didn't even want to mention Mrs. Weatherspoon's name in her presence — and then asked Shannon if she had any ideas.

"Why don't you buy her a present?" Shannon suggested in between bites of her cereal.

Brett frowned. "I don't have much money. I wish I could do some chore for her, like mow her lawn, but she doesn't have much of a lawn anymore!"

"You could offer to run errands for her."

"I guess I could, but that would take up a lot of time." Brett sank down in his chair.

"Geez, Brett," Shannon said. "Do you want to do something for her, or not?"

"Yeah, I do," Brett said. "She's done so much for me, she deserves something really special."

"Why don't you make her something? I bet she'd really like that." Shannon got up to rinse out her cereal bowl.

"What could I make?"

"I don't know. This whole thing was your idea — why don't you figure it out?" She started to leave the room.

"Wait, Shan. Could you help me? You're handy with things."

Shannon cracked a smile. "You trying to butter me up?" She stood up straighter. "Hey, that gives me an idea. You could bake her something."

Brett started to shake his head, then

he thought about it some more. At least it wouldn't take too long.

"Will you help me?" He looked at her pleadingly.

Shannon crossed her arms over her chest. "And what do I get out of this?"

"You can use Cobra all you want," Brett offered.

"I already do. You never ride that thing anymore. You're too busy with The Lizard." She said the board's name with a sneer.

Brett got up and patted her on the back. "How about some brotherly companionship, then?"

"Don't make me sick," Shannon said. But she started to take the flour and sugar canisters out of the cupboard.

Brett laughed at himself for feeling nervous as he stood in front of Mrs. Weatherspoon's door with a tin of freshly baked cookies. Most of the batch had burned — Shannon had blamed him for not paying attention — but they had managed to salvage enough to make a decent offering. She's bound to like them, and anyway, it's the thought that counts, he told himself.

"Well, hello there, Brett," she said when she opened the door. "You're a little early for skateboarding, but I guess it would be all right, just this once . . ."

"That's not why I came over, Mrs. Weatherspoon," he blurted. "I wanted to give you this." He shoved the tin into her hands.

Her eyes opened wide in surprise and then she broke into a smile when she took off the lid. "Chocolate chip — my favorite."

"Mine, too," said Brett, grinning. "I made them for you."

"You did? Why, that was so thoughtful of you, to go to all that trouble, just for me. Would you like to come in and have some?" She held the screen door open for him, and he stepped inside.

"I don't want to bother you," Brett said. "I just wanted to say thank you, for all you've done for us skateboarders. First you built the rink, and now you're putting on a contest . . ."

Mrs. Weatherspoon's smile faded. "About the contest, Brett, I'm afraid I have some bad news. Come here and sit down." She sat on her flowered sofa and patted the cushion next to her.

Brett sat on the edge, feeling his earlier nervousness return.

"It looks as though we're going to have to postpone the contest for a while," she told him sadly.

"Why?" Brett blurted. "What happened?"

Mrs. Weatherspoon leaned back, as if she were tired. "Your friend Thurman did a great job of spreading the word —"

"My friend who?"

"Thurman — the one who knows so much about skateboarding."

"Oh, you must mean W.E.," Brett said with

a short laugh. "We call him Walking Encyclopedia." With a name like Thurman, Brett thought, it's no wonder he uses a nickname.

"Well, he certainly is that. Anyway, he spread the word quickly, and I received a few telephone calls last night. It seems that some of the parents in town aren't so enthusiastic about the idea."

Brett immediately thought of his mother's reaction. She must have put the nix on this, he concluded. She probably called her friends and got them all stirred up. It was just like her. He felt a warm flush rising in his face.

"I can understand their point," Mrs. Weatherspoon went on. "They are concerned about safety, and my liability in case of an accident . . ."

"But that won't happen!" Brett cried, nearly jumping out of his seat. "We'll be careful."

Mrs. Weatherspoon patted his knee and said softly, "No matter how careful you might be, accidents happen." She put on a smile, as if she were trying to cheer him up. "Anyway, that isn't the real problem — I have insurance — but I don't want to go against parents' wishes. I just need more time to get everyone on our side, okay?"

In this town that could take forever, Brett wanted to say, but he remained silent. He was afraid that if he opened his mouth now he might start to cry.

Mrs. Weatherspoon read the disappointment on his face. "Don't worry, Brett. It'll all work out, I'm sure."

Brett felt like a cat trapped in a box, and he wanted to scratch and claw his way out. This time he *did* jump up. He didn't know what he was going to do, but he had to get outside. "I gotta go," he said abruptly, as he strode to the door.

"Thanks again for the cookies, Brett. That was very kind. I'll see you later, when you come back to skate?" She sounded uncertain.

"Yeah, sure," Brett mumbled. He ran down the steps, his eyes blurring.

He swiped the tears off his face angrily. It was so unfair! What did this stupid town have against skateboarding? Why did his family have to move from Ridgeville in the first place? The kids just wanted to have some innocent fun.

But the contest was more than that for Brett, he had to admit. It was going to be the culmination of all his hard work, his chance to achieve his dream. Now he might never get to show people what he could do, to show that he was the best at his chosen sport.

Too bad for him that his chosen sport was one that Springton didn't allow.

Brett slammed the door behind him when he arrived home and sank onto the living room couch. He had no more energy left; he felt like sitting there for the rest of the summer.

"What's with you?" Mrs. Thyson asked as she walked into the room.

She was the last person he wanted to see — much less talk to — right now. "As if you didn't know," he said sullenly.

"I don't know, and that's why I asked," she said, taking a seat in the recliner next to him.

"Well, your little scheme worked."

"I still don't know what you're talking about, Brett, and I don't appreciate your nasty tone." She eyed him fiercely.

Brett didn't care that she was angry. He was angrier. "The skateboarding contest is off — all because of you!" he shouted.

"Wait a minute, Brett, that's a shame, but —"

Brett shot up from his seat. "Don't tell me it's a shame. You wanted this to happen. You couldn't wait to ruin it for me, could you?" With that, Brett raced up the stairs to his room, where he flung himself on his bed.

Brett couldn't bring himself to face The Lizard for the rest of the day, and he spent hours on end in front of the television, not paying much attention to what flickered on the screen. He tried not to think about anything, but every once in a while another wave of disappointment would wash over him, leaving a bitter taste in his mouth.

Fortunately, his parents had to go out that night, so Brett didn't have to face anyone but Shannon at the dinner table. The dark looks he gave her every time she tried to engage him in conversation finally convinced her to leave him alone. She went up to her room to practice her sax, while he plunked himself down in front of the TV again.

Around eight o'clock, the phone rang, bringing Brett out of his stupor.

"Ummm, hello?"

"Brett?"

"Yes. Who's this?"

"It's Johnee. What's up? Why weren't you at Mrs. Weatherspoon's today?"

"I don't know," Brett said. "I guess I just needed a day off."

Johnee chuckled. "You?" Then his voice grew serious again. "We thought you might be upset, you know, about the contest."

Brett was quiet for a moment. "I'm okay."

"Can you come out now?"

"I'm kinda tired. Maybe I'll see you tomorrow."

"Okay, man." Johnee sounded disappointed. "You sure you're okay? We don't need any dumb contest to have fun."

Brett wanted to say, *Maybe you don't need the contest, but I do.* Instead he said, "Yeah. See you."

When he hung up the receiver, he felt more depressed — and alone — than ever.

~ 12 ~

BRETT DIDN'T see his parents again until the next day, when they called him into the living room. Both of them looked very stern, and he felt a lump of dread grow in his stomach. He figured he was going to get it for yelling at his mom, something he now regretted. Still, he couldn't help feeling that they — at least she — didn't understand him at all.

Mr. Thyson started it off. "Brett, we want to talk to you, and we'd like you to hear us out before you say anything. Okay?"

Brett nodded, thinking that he already knew what they were going to say.

"I understand that there was going to be a

skateboarding contest" — he made a vague gesture in the direction of Mrs. Weatherspoon's house — "and you accused your mother of sabotaging it somehow."

Brett didn't answer. He didn't dare to.

"Well, you're wrong. Dead wrong."

"Do you know where we were last night?" he went on, and again Brett didn't bother to reply. "We were at a town council meeting."

Brett wondered what this had to do with him. His father often went to council meetings.

Mr. Thyson looked at his wife. "Actually, we didn't go together. Your mother surprised me by showing up." He turned to Brett. "She surprised me even more when she brought up the subject of this contest."

Brett stared at his mother, open mouthed. This time she really *had* gone out of her way to ruin things for him. Why?

"She convinced the council to put up funds for the contest so that Mrs. Weatherspoon wouldn't have to foot the bill herself," Mr. Thyson stated matter-of-factly.

Brett was confused for a minute. "You mean, the contest is on?"

Mrs. Thyson nodded. "That's right, Brett. The town is going to sponsor it — and provide year-round insurance coverage as well. Now Mrs. Weatherspoon doesn't have to worry about being sued in case of an accident."

Brett couldn't believe his ears. "But, Mom, I thought you were against —"

"I was against the idea of Mrs. Weatherspoon having to hold the contest, not against the contest itself," she explained. "I think this town *should* do something — she's done quite enough on her own."

Brett couldn't agree more. Still, he couldn't understand the apparent change in his mother. "But you hate skateboarding."

Mrs. Thyson reached for his hand. "I don't hate skateboarding. I just don't want to see you get hurt." She smiled warmly. "The other day you said I don't care about you. That's not true at all. If anything, I care too much. I guess that's my problem."

"I'm sorry, Mom," Brett blurted, giving her a hug.

"That's the other thing we wanted to talk to you about," his father interjected, "your recent behavior toward your mother." He glared at Brett, who froze, now afraid that he would be banned from entering the contest.

"I don't want to hear that kind of talk around here again," Mr. Thyson said.

Brett waited to hear the rest, but it seemed his father had finished.

"You won't, I promise," he said contritely. "I'm sorry, Mom," he repeated.

"Well," she said, getting up from the couch, "you better get back on that board and start practicing. You only have a few days."

Brett let out a whoop of joy and hugged her again. "Don't worry, Mom. I'm ready!"

~ ~ ~

The day of the contest started out comfortably enough, but by noon it was a scorcher. Ninety-two degrees was the report over the radio.

Inside the arena Brett saw several kids he knew, and others he didn't know. Kyle and Johnee were there, naturally. They were sitting on the same picnic table bench, but on opposite ends. Which was no surprise. Johnee had as much love for Kyle as Brett did.

The town had done a terrific job arranging the contest. They had even hired a man to announce the events on a public address system. W.E.'s knowledge of skateboarding had earned him a seat right next to the announcer, and Brett knew W.E. was as excited about the event as the actual contestants.

There weren't too many skaters, and only about a dozen spectators, who stood along the fence behind the skaters' benches. But it didn't matter to Brett. All he cared about was the chance to compete officially with Kyle. It was hard to believe that the day had actually arrived!

After a few introductory remarks, the first contestant in the Beginners Division was announced.

"Mickey Roper!"

Several people applauded as a boy about nine, wearing knee and elbow protectors and gloves, got up from a bench on which other contestants about his size were sitting, and put on a helmet. He stepped onto his neon green skateboard and pushed off in a wide circle around the smooth, blacktopped arena.

Brett watched him closely, realizing within seconds that the kid couldn't have been skating more than a couple of weeks. He skated forward rapidly, then shifted his weight to his front foot and lifted the tail of the skateboard into the air, almost losing his balance as he did so. It was an easy maneuver (one of the first Brett had learned, too), but he could see that the boy still had a while to go before he'd get that one down pat.

"That's a G-turn," the announcer explained.

Mickey did a few other tricks, including a Rail Slide — skating parallel to the curb, then lifting the curbside wheels up onto the curb with both trucks resting and sliding on its edge. He lost his balance performing this one and almost took a spill.

Righting himself, he did a Nose Wheelie, skating forward with the tail of his skateboard in the air. Then he skated up a ramp, lifting the front truck over the edge for the start of a Rock 'n' Roll. Balancing himself on the top of the ramp, he rocked back and forth, then leaped off and finished with a Foot Plant, in which he skated up to an empty bench, crouched down to grab the tail of his board, then jumped up on the bench with the board still under his feet. For a moment he made it, then he lost his balance — and his skateboard, which rolled off into the crowd. A whistle blew, announcing that his time was up.

He jumped off the bench and sat down, shaking his head disgustedly. But a resounding cheer rose from the crowd anyway. Brett applauded, too. In spite of his few mistakes, the kid had done okay.

Another name was announced, and another young boy from the same bench got up and performed. And then two girls took their turns.

It was during the fourth contestant's performance — an excellent one — that a familiar voice piped up behind Brett.

"She should've been in the Advanced Division," W.E. said. "She did that Rail Slide like an expert. And she had no problem with the Kick Turn and the Ollie. What do you think, Brett?"

Brett heard the whirring sound of an advancing film, and looked at him. W.E. was snapping pictures.

"I think you're right," he agreed. "But what are you doing here? I thought you were supposed to be sitting with the announcer."

"Oh, he doesn't need me. Besides, this is

where the action is," W.E. replied as he took another shot.

Three other kids were called up to participate in the event, all of whom performed pretty much the same tricks. Brett was amazed at their abilities. He couldn't have done as well when he was their age. But that was before he found The Lizard, he thought, looking appreciatively at the board on the bench next to him.

It was quite obvious who the winner of the Beginners Division would be, he thought, mentally picking the girl he and W.E. had talked about. And they were right. When the winner was announced, Cathy Foster approached the center of the arena and claimed her prize, a gift certificate worth ten dollars.

Isaac Walsh was the first competitor in the Advanced Division, starting off like a house afire. His first move was a 360-degree spin in the air.

"A three-sixty Ollie Kick Flip," the announcer explained. "A tough trick, but Isaac did it perfectly."

The small crowd applauded.

He performed half a dozen other tricks, each time drawing cheers from the crowd.

One after another the contestants were announced, and with each one Brett grew more nervous. What if he made a mistake and ended up on the ground? What if he wasn't better than Kyle?

Brett shook his head firmly. This was no time for doubts. He had The Lizard, after all, and together they were unbeatable.

He pulled the folded-up photocopy of Lance Hawker's picture out of his T-shirt pocket. He had decided to bring it along for luck. Brett visualized himself sailing through the air, just like Crackerjack, with the number six emblazoned on his chest . . .

Only Brett's number was seven. Johnee had six, and Kyle was five. Suddenly Brett got an idea.

124~

He tapped Johnee on the shoulder. "Hey, Johnee."

"Hey, man," Johnee greeted him. "Good show so far, eh?"

"Yeah," Brett agreed. "Listen, I was wondering something — wanna trade places?"

"Whaddaya mean?" Johnee started to get up. "You want to sit here?"

"No, no. I mean, do you want to switch numbers, so I can go right after Kyle?" Brett removed the paper that was taped to his back and handed it to Johnee.

Johnee frowned and didn't take it. "Why can't you wait your turn, like everybody else?"

"Oh, come on, man. What's it to you?" Brett said. "You know this means a lot to me."

"Well, in case you haven't noticed, I'm a contestant, too. Maybe I'd like to keep my spot," Johnee replied.

Brett kept looking over his shoulder so he wouldn't miss Kyle's performance. He knew Kyle would be called any second now.

~ 125

"I'd really appreciate it, Johnee," he said, trying to be patient.

"Why does it matter so much? It's just a number," Johnee said.

"It's more than just a number to me," Brett admitted, though he felt foolish doing so. "It's my lucky number. It was the number Lance Hawker wore."

"And you think that's a *lucky* number?" Johnee scoffed.

Brett didn't have time to explain. "Just give it to me, okay?" And with that he grabbed Johnee's number off his back and started taping it on his own shirt.

"Hey!" cried Johnee. He tried to grab the paper back, but Brett had already moved out of reach. "You're weird, Thyson, you know that?" Johnee called after him.

Brett asked W.E. to inform the announcer of the change, and then he turned to watch the next performer: Kyle Robinson. His attention was riveted on Kyle's feet as he started off with a Kick Turn, skating swiftly up a ramp. At the last moment, just as the nose of the board was ready to leave the ramp, Kyle put his weight on his rear foot, twisted around, and skated back down.

The crowd applauded.

Kyle did a Tail Wheelie, putting both feet on the rear of the board and skating on just the rear wheels. Then he did a Nose Wheelie, which was just the opposite of the Tail Wheelie, followed by a Judo Air, in which one foot stayed on the board and the other did a karate kick forward.

He did this trick several times, alternating the kicks from one foot to the other, and never losing his balance. The crowd cheered. Brett didn't clap. He just watched, wondering if he could copy those moves. He felt sure he could.

Kyle performed other tricks, including a handstand with both hands, and finally — just as the whistle blew — a fantastic jump off the top of a ramp, over a three-foot-high horizontal pole with his feet free of the board, and then landing on the board as it skimmed underneath the pole.

The crowd applauded like crazy, and Brett wondered if he could outdo that. Those last two tricks, no doubt, were Kyle's best.

Then, "Our next contestant, Brett Thyson!" came the announcement over the PA system.

Brett caught his breath and held it. The moment had come. He could hardly believe it. For the first time in his life, he was going to compete in a skateboarding contest.

He stood up as a round of applause greeted him. He put on his helmet, put his foot on the skateboard, and was ready to go.

~ 13 ~

H E STARTED off with some easy tricks first: a Tail Wheelie, a Hang Ten (hanging the toes of both feet over the nose of the skateboard with the rear of the board off the pavement), a Judo Air, and a few others that Kyle and the other contestants had done. Next he did a handstand, using both hands, *then letting go of the board with one hand and standing straight up on the other.*

"Hey, look at that, will you? A Gymnast Plant!" the announcer yelled, surprised and obviously enthusiastic. "Young Brett's the only one who has done that trick so far!"

The crowd showed its surprise and pleasure,

too, cheering and applauding. So far, so good, Brett thought, as he looked forward to other moves he expected to do. He was confident now that he was going to skate the best he had ever skated in his life. Better than anyone else. He was sure he could. That was a promise to himself.

He did a couple of Hippy Twists, 360s, then a 540 — a one-and-a-half twist, landing backwards on the board and not losing his balance one bit.

After taking just a few seconds to catch his breath, he skated down the arena several yards, crouched down on the board, grabbed its ends, and stretched his body out horizontally while the board rolled down the pavement. He had worked on this move dozens of times, but never on a skateboard. It had been on his bedroom floor. It was his first time on a skateboard, and it worked.

He raced up another ramp, and, as he reached the top, grabbed an edge of the skateboard with one hand and the edge of the ramp

with the other, and *somersaulted back onto the pavement.*

The announcer whistled his surprise and awe as the crowd again cheered and applauded. "A Radical Invert," he explained.

Brett did a few wheelies to recover his breath again, a Fast Flowage (skating as fast as he could down the arena, then lifting the board off the pavement for a moment with one foot), then another Hand Plant just as the whistle blew.

Applause filled the air as he wheelied to a dead stop, nodded to the applauding crowd, and headed silently back to the bench.

Two other skaters performed before the contest was over, including Johnee, who did very well but didn't try anything too fancy. After the last skater, the crowd waited in breathless silence for the winner to be announced. Brett, sweat glistening on his face, had his elbows resting on his knees and was gazing at the skateboard between his sneakered feet.

"Think we won it, Lizard?" he said quietly. "Think we won the contest?"

"Ladies and gentlemen, boys and girls, we have a winner," the announcer said. "It's . . . Brett Thyson! Congratulations, Brett! Come up here and claim your gift certificate!"

Once more the crowd cheered and applauded as Brett jumped up, punched the air with his fist, and strode over to the announcer's stand to receive his award. He didn't really care about the prize — this moment of victory was enough.

"Thank you," he said, shaking hands with the presenter.

"I never doubted it one bit," W.E. said, reaching forward to shake his hand, too. "Congratulations, Brett."

"Thanks, W.E.," Brett said. He realized that, except for one shaky moment, he hadn't doubted himself either. He knew he was the best, and now everyone else would know it, too.

He expected Johnee to come over and congratulate him, too, but Johnee was nowhere to be seen. Brett noticed that Kyle also had disappeared. Sore loser, Brett thought, disappointed that he had missed seeing Kyle's reaction to his win.

There were others who did come over: his mother, father, Shannon, and a couple of other people he didn't even know.

"I can't believe it, Brett," his mother said, looking at him as if he had won an Olympic medal. "You were . . . incredible! I never knew you could do tricks like that!"

"Really surprised you, didn't I, Mom?" he said, amused.

"You sure did!" she declared.

"And me, too," his father said, his face wreathed in a smile. "You must have been practicing all those tricks behind our backs."

"Not all of them," he said honestly. "Here, take my prize home with you." He handed the certificate to his father.

Could there really be another reason, other

than pure guts and ability, that he had been able to perform all those tricks? he wondered. It certainly wasn't because he had practiced them. Heck, he didn't even know half of the tricks he had done, or their names! They had just come to him while he was riding the skateboard!

So . . . what was truly behind his prize-winning performance? His *natural* ability? Or was it The Lizard?

The Lizard, heck, he told himself. It's my natural ability. It is!

Brett waited for the crowd to disperse, then went up to Mrs. Weatherspoon, who'd been congratulating all of the contestants and their parents.

"That was great, Mrs. Weatherspoon," he said. "We all appreciate what you did very much."

Mrs. Weatherspoon's face spiderwebbed into a broad smile as she took Brett's hand and shook it. "Well, it's nice to be able to help the kids in the neighborhood," she said. "You did very well, Brett. Amazingly well, as a matter of fact."

"Thanks," he said. "Well, see you later, Mrs. Weatherspoon," he added, and pushed off on his skateboard.

He left the yard, skated out to the street, and headed for home.

He put The Lizard in the garage and went into the house. He had barely closed the kitchen door behind him when he received an unexpected ovation. "Guess who came in first in the Advanced Division of the skateboard contest! Our one and only . . . Brett Thyson!"

He stood, still panting, as Shannon rushed up to him and gave him a big hug. Standing behind her, her face flushed with admiration, too, was Kristyne Medler.

When Shannon broke away from him, Kristyne gave him a hug, too, though not a bear one like Shannon's. "You were fantastic, Brett," she said, stepping back and looking at him. "I never dreamed anybody could do the tricks you did."

136~

He grinned, and shrugged. "It just takes practice," he said modestly. But, in his case, was it only practice? he asked himself. The question didn't want to go away. Those accidents, and near-accidents . . .

"When do we eat?" he asked, forcing a laugh as he turned to his mother.

She smiled. "Can you wait fifteen minutes, champ?"

"I can wait," he said, and gave her a hug.

A couple of mornings later, a little after ten o'clock, Brett got tired of just sitting around the house and went out to ride The Lizard. He'd done a couple of chores — swept off the walks and cleaned out the crawl space underneath the house — and was getting restless. Now that the contest was over he felt let down. He just had to get out and do something, and nothing would make him feel better right now than riding around on The Lizard.

He waved to the mail carrier coming up the walk, then was attracted by some familiar noises coming from down the street. Sensing action in the offing, he headed in that direction.

Around the corner, a small, two-story house was being lifted from its foundation to be placed onto a flat-bottomed truck. Skateboarding on the street in front of it were Johnee Kale and a couple of other kids.

"Hi, guys," Brett called as he wheelied to a stop in front of them.

"Hi, Brett," the two boys with Johnee answered him. But Johnee just gave him an unpleasant look and skated away. Brett couldn't believe it. Johnee was mad at him! Brett guessed that it had to do with taking his number at the contest.

Geez, Brett thought. Can't he understand that it was important to me? What difference did it make, anyway?

"Okay, boys, take off," a man wearing a white helmet said to them as he came from behind the moving house. "It's dangerous here."

Brett walked out into the street, glancing back and forth to see if cars were coming. He and the other kids waited for two to pass by, then skated to the intersection, where all the kids except Brett turned left. He turned right. Might as well head back for home, he decided.

He skated for a while in front of his house, doing some of the easier tricks — if his mother saw him pulling off some of the fancier free-style stunts now she might fly off the handle — then left The Lizard on the walk and went into the house.

"That you, Brett?" his mother called him from the living room.

"Yeah," he answered.

"Look on the table," she said. "There's a postcard for you."

He saw it, picked it up, and read it. It was printed in ink.

"Lizard Boy, put that skateboard back where you got it from, or you'll be sorrier than ever. Lance Hawker."

~14~

"**I** SAW that note," his mother said. "Who's Lance Hawker?"

Brett reread the card, feeling an icy chill starting at the base of his spine and working upward.

"Did you hear me?" she repeated. "Who's Lance Hawker?"

A deep frown appeared on Brett's forehead. "The guy who used to own The Lizard," he said, his voice so low it was barely audible.

"How do you know that?"

"W.E. told me."

"How does he know?"

"W.E. knows a lot of things," Brett said, and went into the next room, feeling like squashing the postcard into a lump in his hand. But he didn't. He had to keep it for proof. He was going to show it to W.E., call him a rotten, dirty rat for writing him such a note, and shove it down his throat. Because nobody except W.E. had ever said that The Lizard was hexed. Nobody. It had to be him.

"Maybe you should rebury it, Brett," Shannon's voice came from the chair by the window. She was studying one of her music sheets.

He glared at her. "Rebury it? Why? You crazy or something?"

"No. But ever since you've had The Lizard you . . ." She shrugged her shoulders, as if she were having trouble saying what she wanted to say.

"Yeah, go on," Brett said, a slight bit of anger in his voice. "Ever since I've had it . . . what?"

"You haven't been the same," she said, looking directly at him. "You've been a different person. You've not only become a real whiz on that skateboard, but it seems — I don't know — it seems to have gone to your head."

Her eyes were wide now, as if she thought she'd gone too far.

"You *are* crazy, Shan," Brett snapped. "How could I be a different person just because of a new skateboard? That's movie stuff. Cartoon stuff." He laughed at her as he held up the postcard. "You don't really believe that this was written by Lance Hawker, do you? The guy's dead! No dead guy can write a postcard! I know who wrote it, just as well as I know my own name! It was W.E.! He's the only guy who'd do a rotten thing like this!"

"Why?" she asked. "Why would W.E. do it?"

Brett's eyes narrowed, and his mouth tightened into a thin, hard line. "Because he thinks it's hexed, that's why. Isn't that stupid?"

She closed the music book and stood up. "I don't know," she answered, heading out of the room. "I just know that it's done *something* to you, that's all."

She disappeared down the hallway, and a moment later Brett heard her bedroom door close.

Brett mulled over his sister's words. Well, maybe he *had* changed. When you begin performing tricks on a skateboard that you've never performed before in your life, you're bound to change a little, aren't you?

One thing for certain: he wasn't going to rebury The Lizard, no matter what she, and that postcard, said.

But there was one thing he was going to do, and he was going to do it now. He went to the telephone, picked up the directory, found W.E.'s number, and dialed it.

"You're a rat, W.E.," he said the minute he recognized W.E.'s familiar, high-pitched voice. "You know that? Writing that postcard is the lowest, meanest thing a guy could do, and I . . ." He was so angry that even the receiver was trembling. "I don't want to speak to you again."

He was about to hang up. But W.E. said,

"What postcard? What are you talking about, Brett? I didn't send you any postcard."

"Don't lie to me. Only you would've written a note like that."

"You're way out of line, Brett. I haven't written a postcard since Christmas. What did it say?"

"*You* know what it said." Again he was about to hang up, but the way W.E. was answering him . . .

"I don't, Brett," W.E. said, his voice soft, sincere. "Honest. I don't have the faintest idea what you're talking about. Why are you so sure I wrote it? Is it in my handwriting? Because if it is, somebody forged it. And I don't know who'd do a dirty, dumb thing like that."

Brett stared at the wall a minute, suddenly wondering if he was wrong after all. He hadn't thought about the handwriting. And the writing wasn't in longhand. It was printed.

No, he wasn't sure it was W.E.'s handwriting. And, because of the sincerity of W.E.'s voice . . .

Darn it, he *believed* W.E. Somebody else must have written that postcard. Who? Kyle Robinson?

"I'm sorry, W.E.," he said, embarrassed and apologetic. "I'm really sorry. I . . . I don't know what else to say."

"That's okay. What did the card say?" W.E. asked.

"Something about my reburying The Lizard, and it was signed by Lance Hawker."

"Oh. And because I've been telling you about Lance you figured I was the guilty party."

"I guess that's it. I'm sorry, W.E." He was about to hang up for the third time, and thought of something. "Did you say anything about The Lizard to Kyle?"

There was a momentary silence, then W.E. answered. "I don't know, Brett. I don't think so, but I'm not sure. Why? You think . . . ?"

"I'm not sure what to think," Brett replied, confused. "Thanks, W.E. See you later."

This time he hung up.

Had Kyle learned about the background of The Lizard from someone? From W.E.?

Should he call up Kyle and bluntly ask him? That would be a waste of time, he decided. Even if Kyle knew about The Lizard he wouldn't admit that he had written the postcard. He'd just get a big laugh out of it.

No, he might as well forget about it. Forget the whole thing. Why let the postcard bother him? They were just words. They meant nothing . . . nothing at all. Someone was just trying to get his goat, that was all.

He tore up the card and tossed the pieces into the kitchen trash can.

Without saying anything to his mother he went back outside. He had to do something to get that miserable postcard out of his mind, even if the warning on it was stupid. And there was no better way than . . .

He glanced at the spot where he had left The Lizard. It wasn't there.

For a minute, surprise and worry clutched his chest like tentacles of steel as his eyes darted around the yard. Darn! What could've . . . ?

He heard a shout, and looked up the street.

A window had slipped out of a carpenter's hands as he was trying to lift it into a building, and it was falling toward the pavement, where a kid was skateboarding!

It didn't take Brett more than a second to recognize the kid — and the skateboard.

~ 15 ~

CRASH!

If Kyle hadn't reacted as quickly as he had, and swerved out of the way just in time, the window would have landed right on top of him. It could have killed him.

Brett stood there for a moment, paralyzed with shock — shock over the near-accident, and shock over Kyle's taking The Lizard. Kyle had lifted it right off Brett's front yard. If that wasn't the most brazen, rotten thing anybody could do . . . And yet, despite his anger, Brett was relieved when Kyle rose to his feet, apparently unhurt.

"You okay?" yelled the guy up on the ladder as he started to make a hasty descent.

"Yeah," Kyle answered, brushing off his pants. He clutched his own skateboard, as if it were his most prized possession, too.

"Hey, Kyle!" Brett shouted when he could move. "What did you think you were doing?" He dashed into the street to retrieve The Lizard, which had skittered out from under Kyle when he fell.

Brett picked it up and approached Kyle, but Kyle got on his own skateboard and started skating away.

"Come back here, Robinson!" Brett called after him. "You're a real jerk! A thief! Know what? That window should have hit you! Then you wouldn't be stealing skateboards! You wouldn't write nasty postcards!"

At the word "postcards," Kyle paused and looked back at him.

"Postcards?"

"Yes, postcards! And don't tell me you don't know what I'm talking about!"

"I don't," Kyle said. He frowned and looked perplexed.

"You didn't send me that card? You didn't sign it Lance Hawker?"

"No."

Brett stared at him. "I don't believe you. Why should I believe a thief?"

Kyle shrugged. "Believe what you want. I didn't send you any card. And I didn't steal your skateboard — I just wanted to try it out for a minute."

Brett put his hand on his hip. "Yeah, sure. And then you were going to bring it right back."

"Yeah, I was. I couldn't keep it — everybody knows that board is yours, especially now, after the contest."

Kyle's face remained stony, but Brett guessed that Kyle was envious of Brett's recent win. He should be! thought Brett.

"Knowing you, you'd steal The Lizard, paint it so no one could recognize it, and then use it to win the next contest," Brett accused him.

Kyle's eyes narrowed into slits, and he replied calmly, "I don't have to depend on a board to win a contest."

Kyle spun and pushed off, the trucks and wheels of his skateboard rasping in his wake.

For a while Brett watched him, still unsure about whether to believe him.

"He take your skateboard, kid?" the carpenter asked as he gathered up the shards of glass all over the sidewalk.

"Yeah," said Brett.

"He almost got punished for it," the carpenter commented. "That was a close call." He glanced back at the ladder he had been standing on and wiped his brow in relief.

Brett just nodded and then headed for home, this time wondering: If Kyle didn't write the postcard, and W.E. didn't write it, who did?

Another thought began to weigh on his mind, too, a thought that got heavier and heavier every minute.

Wasn't it funny, or was it just a coincidence, that Kyle had taken The Lizard, and then, only seconds later, was almost struck by a falling window?

Goosebumps popped up on his arms. This time it was harder than ever to erase the grim thought from his mind.

Two Saturdays later, the town sponsored another skateboarding contest at Mrs. Weatherspoon's arena. This one was advertised in various places, including Cole's Sporting Goods store, which volunteered to contribute to the awards.

This time there would be three winners in each division, the Beginners and the Advanced, and the contest was designated a streetstyle skateboarding contest.

Brett felt proud. He had started it all, with his letter. He and good ol' Mrs. Weatherspoon, who had done something about it.

The benches for the Advanced Division contestants were full by the time Brett arrived, so he stood behind the others, holding his skateboard at his side.

One by one he watched the skaters in the Beginners Division do their routines, then clapped when they were finished and the first three winners were announced.

Then came the Advanced Division, and he watched his friends perform tricks he had seen dozens of times before and whose difficulty he appreciated, but inwardly he knew he had done them better. Much better.

Both Johnee Kale and Kyle Robinson performed before he did. Each did a great job, and drew resounding cheers.

Finally, "Brett Thyson!" the announcer called over the loudspeaker.

The cheer that rose for him was twice as loud as any other. His body shook. His heart pounded. He stepped around the benches, put down his skateboard, placed a foot on it, and pushed off. He did a Kick Turn, a Shoot the

Duck, an Ollie, then went into a two-handed handstand, and *fell*.

The crowd groaned. "Oh, no!" Brett heard a spectator cry out.

He restored his balance quickly, did a few other simple tricks, then thought of making up for that goof by doing a Hand Plant, maybe following that up with a launch off the ramp and a complete 360. But a strange feeling washed over him like a flood of ice-cold water. *He couldn't do it. He knew he couldn't, and there was no sense trying. He'd just make a fool of himself and maybe get hurt.*

He continued with the simple tricks that he was familiar with, waiting for the whistle to end his unspectacular performance.

Finally, it blew. Relieved, he wheelied to a stop and rushed off to the side. The applause was a tenth of what it had been when he was introduced.

"What happened, Brett?" a dozen voices rose from the disappointed crowd. "What happened to the great tricks you did the last time?"

He didn't answer.

At last the contest was over and the winners were announced. "First prize winner! A thirty-five-dollar gift certificate to . . . Kyle Robinson!"

Cheers rose from the crowd.

Brett wasn't surprised. Kyle was the best. He cheered along with the crowd.

"Second prize winner! A twenty-five-dollar gift certificate to . . . Johnee Kale!"

Another thunder of applause.

Then, "Third prize winner! A five-dollar gift certificate to . . . Ellen Brostek!"

More applause.

"That's it, folks!" the announcer said. "Let's give a big round of applause this time to Mrs. Rita Weatherspoon for allowing us to use her backyard, and for cosponsoring this skateboard contest!"

He motioned to Mrs. Weatherspoon to

stand, and another thunder of applause filled the air as she rose from her chair on the porch.

As Brett joined in the applause, a hand gripped his arm.

"Hey, Lizard Boy! What happened? Where is it? What did you do with The Lizard?"

Brett whirled. *Lizard Boy?* His heart jumped.

"It was *you!*" he said, pressing a finger against Johnee Kale's chest. "*You're* the one who sent me that postcard!"

Johnee smiled and nodded. "Yeah, it was me," he admitted.

"Why? Why did you do it? To scare me?"

"To put some sense into you," Johnee said. "You're my friend, Brett, and I didn't want things to go on as they were between us. Ever since you dug up that skateboard you've been acting weird, like you were possessed by it or something. I wanted you to come back and join the living again. Okay?"

Brett scowled for a moment, then quickly broke into a grin. "You're a pal, Johnee. I'm sorry if I've been a little crazy lately."

Johnee looked relieved. "So, what *did* you do with The Lizard?"

"I did what you told me to do with it — I put it back where it came from."

"You reburied it? Really?" Johnee's eyes sparkled. "That postcard really did the trick."

"Actually, it was Kyle." Brett laughed at Johnee's confused expression. "He got me to thinking that I was relying too much on The Lizard to win for me. I wanted to see if I could do it on my own."

Johnee cast his eyes down and said in a low voice, "I guess you got your answer today, huh?" He looked up at Brett again. "Do you think The Lizard really *was* hexed, like W.E. said?"

Brett shrugged. "It did seem different out there today, without The Lizard. I wasn't as sure of myself. But it could be that I just have to get used to my old board again. I'll know better once I've had more time to practice. Maybe I'll do better next time; maybe I won't. But there's one thing I *do* know . . ."

"What's that?" Johnee asked.

"I'm glad to be rid of that board!" Brett said. He held out his hand and Johnee slapped it.

"All right!" said Johnee. Then he held out his hand and Brett slapped it.

Slowly, they started to head for the exit when a high, shrill voice called, "Brett! Johnee!"

"Guess Mrs. Weatherspoon wants to see us," Johnee said.

Maybe she wants to tell me how lousy I performed, Brett thought. As if I didn't know.

They stitched their way through the small crowd to the steps leading up to the porch where Mrs. Weatherspoon was standing, and smiled up at her.

"Hi, Mrs. Weatherspoon," Johnee said. "It was a great contest, wasn't it? And we really owe it all to you. Every bit of it."

"That goes for me, too, Mrs. Weatherspoon," Brett said.

The wrinkles around her eyes creased as she smiled and extended her hands to the boys.

Each took a hand — Brett her right one and Johnee her left — and held it warmly, as she held theirs.

"I just want to tell you, Brett, how much I owe you for having written that letter and giving me an opportunity to do something for a lot of the boys and girls in this neighborhood. Most of all, I want to thank you for something else."

She paused, and Brett felt her hand squeeze his even a little tighter.

"What's that, Mrs. Weatherspoon?"

"You can't guess?"

He thought about it a minute, but he couldn't.

"I'm sorry. I guess I can't . . ."

"Think about Kyle a minute. Kyle Robinson," she said, and looked at him closely.

Then it dawned on him. Yes, he knew exactly what she meant, now.

"You're right, Mrs. Weatherspoon," he said. "I don't think you have to worry about him and me anymore. I wanted to show him what I could do, and I did, at the last contest. Today he won fair and square."

"Your frustrations are over as far as Kyle Robinson is concerned?"

He nodded. "Yes, ma'am. He's a good skater, and I know I can be, too. For now, though, I just want to have fun with it!"

Mrs. Weatherspoon's eyes shifted to Johnee's, and she shook her head. "Guess Kyle wasn't the only one we were concerned about, was he, Johnee?"

Johnee laughed. "I guess not, Mrs. Weatherspoon," he said.

Brett looked at him, and laughed, too. He knew exactly what they were referring to — his and Johnee's own friendship. It had been on the edge of disaster, just because of the way he had talked and acted. All because of The Lizard.

Mrs. Weatherspoon glanced over their heads. "Well," she observed, "the crowd's all gone.

And I suppose you two want to get home and satisfy your empty stomachs, too. See you later, okay?"

"Okay, Mrs. Weatherspoon," they said in unison. They jumped off the porch, got on their skateboards, and skated away.

"She's terrific, isn't she?" Johnee cried as they skated out onto the sidewalk.

"More than terrific," said Brett. "She's super-terrific!"

At the intersection they split, Johnee turning left and Brett heading straight ahead.

"Welcome home, Cobra," Brett said, smiling down at his skateboard.